Four Hidden Treasures

Four Hidden Treasures

A Secrets of Hartwell Novel

H L Marsay

TULE
PUBLISHING

The human heart has hidden treasures,
In secret kept, in silence sealed;
The thoughts, the hopes, the dreams, the pleasures,
Whose charms were broken if revealed.

Charlotte Brontë 1816–1855
Yorkshire

CHAPTER ONE

L UCY STOOD IN the ballroom of Hartwell Hall and watched as a drop of water trickled down the wall, leaving a dark trail on the red silk wallpaper. She looked up just in time for another drop to hit her straight in the eye.

"Bloody place! The roof's turned into a sieve." She sighed as she placed a saucepan on the polished wood floor with only a second to spare before the next heavy drop plopped in. She cast a careful eye over the ceiling once more before stepping out of the ballroom and into the long corridor that led back to the main hall. She dodged past two more pans and a bucket. It was always the same when it rained heavily: a mad dash to catch all the leaks. The latest estimate for fixing the roof had arrived that morning. It lay discarded on the kitchen table amongst the empty coffee cups and bills waiting to be paid. Fifty thousand pounds, and that was only for the west wing. Well, it would have to wait, along with all the other repairs and maintenance work Hartwell Hall needed.

When she arrived in the grand reception hall, she found yet another bucket, full to the brim and overflowing on to the black and white marble floor. With a groan she carried it into the cloakroom, trying not to mind as the cold water sloshed on to her jeans. Then she emptied the water down the sink, before returning the bucket to its position at the bottom of the sweeping cantilever staircase. Lucy stood and gazed at the stairs for a second. Over nine years ago, she'd posed there for a photograph on her wedding day, in her huge white dress. Standing there with her blonde hair piled on her head and the Hanley tiara holding her impossibly long veil in place as it trailed out behind her, Rupert smiling by her side. She had been so happy that day. The photo had appeared in *Tatler*. 'Rupert and Lucinda, the new Lord and Lady Hanley, on the occasion of their marriage'. When she'd made her vows in front of their friends and family, she could never have imagined how her life would turn out.

As she walked away from the staircase, she caught sight of her reflection in the ornate gilt mirror hanging on the wall and cringed. Her mascara had streaked down her cheek and there was at least two inches of dark growth at her roots. These days she looked like she belonged on a wanted poster, not the pages of a society magazine. She pushed that thought out of her head and ran her finger beneath her blue eyes to wipe away the smudged make-up and tried fluffing up her hair. Yet another thing to thank Covid for. The hairdressers had been closed for months and now they were open again, it was impossible to get an appointment. Not that she had a hundred quid to throw away on highlights and a cut right now.

The estate had been struggling financially even before the pandemic. When Rupert had first brought her here, she'd immediately fallen in love with the place. Nestled on the edge of the North York Moors, the beautiful Georgian house built in mellow stone—with its porticoed entrance and elegant columns—was a world away from her father's modern Chelsea apartment she'd grown up in. Hartwell Hall had been in Rupert's family for hundreds of years and she could hardly believe she was going to live there with her handsome new husband. Back then of course, she'd had no idea how much it cost to keep the place running. She'd had to learn fast when Rupert disappeared. Ironically, the last time she'd seen him was on that fateful night in March 2020, when the prime minister had addressed the nation and told them all to stay at home.

Since then, she'd had months alone to try and come up with a plan as bills kept arriving and her income continued to dwindle. Finally, she'd decided that as soon as the first lockdown was lifted, she would open the house to the public. Caroline, her mother-in-law, had been horrified at the idea.

"You can't have strangers traipsing through the house, gawping at all your belongings," she had declared, but Lucy didn't mind one bit. However, as it turned out, continued restrictions meant she could only open the grounds. Still, scores of visitors had arrived desperate to enjoy the rose garden, woodland walk, and lawns sweeping down to the lake after being cooped up for months. They had all seemed quite surprised that Lady Hanley, dressed in jeans and wellies, was there to greet them herself and happy to chat away about the house and its history. Lucy enjoyed it. She liked to be kept busy and meeting new people. More importantly the ticket sales had provided a welcome source of income, but then lockdown two had come along. She'd had to close her gates and there had been no income from the holiday cottages either. Most of her tenants in the village had suffered too, with rents either arriving late or not at all, yet the costs of running the estate kept on adding up.

She leaned her head against one of the cool marble pillars and ran her finger along the delicately carved flutings.

"Gosh," she sighed. "I know you are beautiful, but you are high-maintenance."

In the corner, the long case clock struck three o'clock. Lucy checked it against her own watch and groaned. Now she was going to be late to collect Freddie. She dashed back down the corridor accompanied by a little symphony of splishes and splashes from the raindrops. In the kitchen, she grabbed her car keys from their hook only to remember the red light had started flashing on her petrol gauge. The last thing she needed was to break down in the middle of the village.

"Bugger, bugger, bugger!" she muttered as she pulled on her wellies and coat. She'd have to walk there now...or rather run. Thankfully, the rain had finally stopped when she stepped outside. Banging the door shut behind her, she crunched down the long gravel driveway and turned right through the huge wrought-iron gates decorated with the oak tree and white hart of the Hanley family crest. As she passed the gatehouse, she tapped on the window and gave Joan, who as usual was busy baking, a friendly wave. Joan was married to Bill, the estate's gardener. They had lived in the gatehouse for over thirty years and Lucy would be totally lost without them.

The village was a little way up the hill. A collection of about fifty stone-built cottages and houses clustered around a winding stream. She hurried along the cobbled path passing the pub, the church, and the village shop, waving to other parents who were better timekeepers than her. When she finally arrived at the school gates she was quite out of breath. Freddie was waiting for her with Rachel, Lucy's best friend and Freddie's teacher. Rachel was short and stocky with her dark hair pulled back and worn in a long plait. A dependable pit pony next to Lucy's flighty thoroughbred.

"I'm so, so sorry I'm late, darling. Sorry, Rach, I was on bucket duty," Lucy gasped.

"We were about to call you?" said Rachel slipping her mobile back into her satchel. "Everything okay?"

"Has Tilly had her puppies yet, Mum?" asked Freddie hopefully. Lucy grinned at her son and ruffled his blond hair. He was a serious, sensible little boy, and he adored the dogs.

"No, darling, she hasn't, but it won't be long now. When I left, she was fast asleep next to the Aga."

"Good, I don't want to miss it. Please can I get some sweets?" he asked.

Lucy hesitated for a second, Freddie always got a treat from the shop on Fridays, but in her rush, she'd forgotten her purse. Waving away Rachel's silent offer of help, she shoved her hands in her jeans pocket and miraculously found a scrunched-up five-pound note that had quite possibly also been through the washing machine. She smoothed it out and placed it into Freddie's small, outstretched hand.

"Will you be okay on your own?" she asked, although the shop was only a few steps away. Freddie smiled up at her.

"Of course, Mum, thanks."

"How's he been today?" asked Lucy quietly, as she watched him go. Rachel smiled and gave Lucy's arm a reassuring squeeze.

"He's fine, Luce. He's just a quiet kid and like all the ones who were stuck doing home schooling for months on end, he's taking time to adjust to being back in the classroom full-time. Academically, he is way ahead of the others. I'll let him tell you his score, but today's maths test went really well."

"Good, when Caroline hears she might get off my case about sending him to a prep school. I swear the next time she says something, I shall tell her I have no intention of sending Freddie boarding at eight years old. It's barbaric."

Rachel cupped her hand to her ear. "Shh, can you hear that?" she asked.

"What?" Lucy looked around in confusion.

Rachel pointed across the road to the church. "The sound of generations of Hanleys turning in their graves."

"Ha ha very funny." Lucy laughed.

Rachel grinned. "Are you still on for tonight?" she asked. Since lockdown had been lifted, the two of them had got into a routine of going to the pub every Friday, for quiz night.

"Absolutely," replied Lucy, "I'm looking forward to it. Actually, before the stupid rainstorm arrived, I was having a decent day. Max called this morning to say he's found new tenants for Rose and Lilac cottages."

Rachel gave Lucy a pat on the shoulder. "Hey that's fantastic, and it's about time my drip of a brother-in-law did something useful. Things are finally looking up. I told you they would eventually."

Just then the bell on the shop door jangled and Freddie appeared again looking very pleased with himself. He clutched his bag of jelly beans in one hand and his change in the other.

"Here you are, Mum. The sweets were one pound and ten pence, so your change is three pounds and ninety pence," he said as he dropped the coins into Lucy's hand.

"Thank you, darling. How was Mrs Parkin? Did you remember to say please and thank you?"

"Yes, but she was still a bit grumpy. She asked me if I had clean hands, then said she liked it more when everybody had to wear face masks and that if I eat all these sweets my teeth will fall out," replied Freddie looking very serious.

"What a ray of sunshine that woman is," drawled Rachel. "There should be a sign above the shop door: 'Here resides Nora Parkin, Hartwell's biggest gossip and prophet of doom'." She turned to go. "I'll see you later, Luce. Have a lovely weekend, Freddie."

"Thank you, Rachel, I mean Miss Foxton," replied Freddie politely. He often got confused about what to call her.

"See you later," Lucy called after her, before taking her little boy's hand and walking back down the hill. Freddie chattered away and Lucy tried not to let it bother her that he didn't mention school and instead concentrated on his favourite subject.

"Mum, if you could be a dinosaur, which one would you be?"

"Ooh let me think. Which is the one with a long neck?"

"A diplodocus or an apatosaurus," replied Freddie immediately.

"Then I'd be one of those. What about you?"

"A triceratops of course," said Freddie as if there could ever be any doubt in his answer.

"Of course," agreed Lucy.

"Can I go and make a wish?"

They had drawn level with the avenue of ancient oak trees that led down to the well which, along with the deer that roamed free, gave the village its name. There was a legend that the Druids, who had lived in the area thousands of years ago, had thought that the well was sacred. Today the villagers simply called it the wishing well and generations of the young and not so young cast their pennies into the water in the hope that their wishes would be granted.

"Yes, you may," Lucy replied. She handed over a ten-pence piece and followed him as he chased towards the crumbling stone wall surrounding the old well. She stopped and watched as he closed his eyes tight and screwed up his face. She saw his lips moving quickly and silently before he flung the coin down, then waited for the satisfying splash before racing back to her.

"I'm sorry, but I can't tell you what I wished for, or it won't come true," he explained breathlessly.

"I understand," Lucy replied forcing herself to smile. She wasn't sure she wanted to know. What if his wish was about Rupert coming back? He barely ever mentioned his father. Rupert had been away a lot even before he disappeared and when he was at home, Lucy had felt like she was walking on eggshells. He had spent very little time with Freddie, distracted by his other interests, but surely Freddie must miss his father.

As they arrived at the entrance gates to Hartwell Hall, a black Range Rover pulled up alongside them. The window glided down, to reveal a man with a round, slightly ruddy face and greying hair. It was Guy Lovell, the local MP. He had taken over the constituency when Rupert's father died and lived in the village at The Grange. Although he was almost twenty years older than Lucy, she had always found him rather charming, but Rachel thought he was a creep.

"Good afternoon, Lady Hanley. You're looking as lovely as ever," he said beaming at her.

Lucy smiled back, knowing full well she looked a mess. "Hello, Guy, how are you?"

"You know me, busy, busy. I've just been to Thirsk races for the first meeting of the year. It was good to see the place bustling again. Incidentally, I was given a tip for the five-fifteen. False Friend, he's meant to be a dead cert."

Lucy wrinkled her nose. "That's not a very nice name for a horse."

"You're quite right," agreed Guy, with a grin. "Maybe that's why it's fifty to one."

At that moment, a Volvo stopped behind the Range Rover and beeped its horn loudly.

"I think that's my cue to leave. Enjoy your weekend," said Guy before zooming off. His place was taken by the Volvo's driver, dressed in her uniform of tweed skirt, silk twinset, and pearls. Caroline may now live in the dower house, but she still gave the impression that she was in charge of Hartwell Hall and its inhabitants.

"I hope you aren't encouraging him, Lucinda. Think how it might look given your circumstances."

Lucy felt herself flush under the disapproving gaze of her mother-in-law's cold, blue eyes. "He was only being friendly," she stammered.

Caroline arched an eyebrow. "He was flirting," she declared, before turning her attention to Freddie, whose little face looked worried as his eyes flicked between his mother and grandmother. "How are you, Alfred? Did you have a good day at school?"

"Yes thanks, Granny. I got ten out of ten in my maths test today."

Caroline's stony expression cracked into a smile. "Excellent! All our hard work is paying off." Caroline had insisted on being involved with Freddie's home schooling via Zoom each day. "You must come to tea one day next week—not Monday though, I'm playing bridge with Colonel Marsden and the vicar. I'll leave it to your mother to try and organise something. Goodbye, darling."

Caroline wound up her window and drove off without another word to Lucy.

"Bye, Granny." Freddie waved, and Lucy had to stop herself using a very different hand gesture as Caroline's car disappeared over the hill. She was definitely going to put that bet on now.

THEY ARRIVED HOME, to be greeted loudly by Tilly, the Labrador, and Pickle, the Jack Russell. Lucy made Freddie an early supper of beans on toast while he did his homework at the kitchen table. She knew when Joan and Bill arrived to babysit, they would come armed with Tupperware containers full of homemade cakes and buns for her son to gorge on. Then with Freddie and the dogs curled up on the sofa together watching cartoons in the study, she dashed upstairs to shower and change. She slipped into a red maxi dress she hadn't worn in ages and teamed it with her favourite denim jacket. Having carefully applied some lip gloss and mascara and added her favourite earrings, she cast a critical eye over her reflection. It had been ages since she'd worn anything except jeans, but all things considered, she didn't look too bad.

Downstairs the commotion from the dogs told her that Joan and Bill had arrived. Before she left, she checked her phone for the results from Thirsk and gave a whoop of joy. Good old False Friend! Maybe Rachel was right: her luck was changing.

THE WHITE HART was buzzing with the sound of laughter and local gossip when Lucy arrived. It seemed like the whole village was there. If the church was the soul of Hartwell, then the pub was definitely its heart. A long low stone building with beamed ceilings, uneven floors, and small casement windows, it had once been a coaching inn for travellers on their way to York, but now acted as the social centre for village life.

Rachel was leaning across the bar chatting to Jack, the landlord. The two of them had grown up in the village together. Jack had once had a promising career as a rugby player, but a knee injury ended it abruptly and left him with nothing but a limp and a broken nose. He'd come home to help his mother, Shirley, run the pub and now his waistline was almost as wide as his shoulders. However, whatever he lacked in good looks, his good humour more than made up for. During lockdown he had almost single-handedly kept the villagers' spirits up providing takeaway meals, drinks, and his ridiculous online pub quiz every Friday evening. Lockdown was over, but Jack's stint as a quizmaster lived on. He and Rachel both turned and smiled as Lucy made her way to the bar.

"There you are. I'm getting the drinks in. G&T, right?" asked Rachel. She had changed into jeans and her favourite loose-fitting paisley top.

"Yes, please, and supper is definitely on me. I've had a win on the gee-gees. I stuck a tenner on a fifty-to-one tip Guy gave me," announced Lucy proudly.

Rachel raised her eyebrows at the name of the local MP but said nothing.

"Just think," continued Lucy, "if I'd put a hundred quid on it, I'd have fifty grand. That's enough to fix the roof."

Rachel and Jack exchanged a glance.

"No, you wouldn't, Luce," said Jack gently, "you'd have five grand."

"Really? Oh well it would still be a start." She sighed as her friends shook their heads in despair.

"I don't know if I'd be gadding about, enjoying myself if I didn't know where my husband was," said a snide voice from the other side of the bar. Lucy turned her head and flushed when she saw Nora Parkin's sour face, framed with a tight perm, scowling at her.

"Then it's a good thing we all know where your husband is," retorted Rachel immediately leaping to Lucy's defence, "with that pretty young blonde he left you for ten years ago. And who can blame him."

Now it was Nora who had turned red, a picture of indignation.

"Oh, you've a nasty tongue in your head, Rachel Foxton. To think we entrust our children to your care. If your father…"

At this point, Jack stepped in and held up his hands as if to separate the two women.

"Rachel, Nora, please it's been a difficult time for all of us," he began.

"Hear, hear well said, Jack," joined in Reverend Davenport, who had suddenly appeared. He was looking fatter and balder than ever. "Ladies, let our sufferings unite us as one, not tear us apart." He beamed at them both before shuffling back to his table in the corner, glass of whisky in hand.

Lucy and Rachel took their own drinks and sat down at the table in the window that Jack had reserved for them. Lucy's phone bleeped and as she stared at the screen, she began to chew her lower lip, the tell-tale sign that she was worried.

"What's up?" asked Rachel. "You're not going to let that old bag get to you, are you?"

Lucy shook her head. "No, it's not her. I've just got another email from Max with all the details of the new tenants."

"And?"

"The first is a Dr. Meera Kumar. She's going to be our new GP apparently."

"Good, it's about time Robertson retired. He was worse than useless with Dad. I swear he still thinks a spoonful of castor oil is the answer to any ailment."

"Sssh, he'll hear you," whispered Lucy, nodding to the old doctor who was sitting with his back to them.

Rachel shrugged. "Who's renting the other one?" she asked.

Lucy slipped her phone back into her pocket and lowered her voice again. "A Detective Sergeant Ormond who's transferring here from London." She paused. "Do you think we should be worried?"

Rachel took a sip of her wine, and firmly shook her head. "No of course not. Loads of people have decided to move to the countryside, looking for a better life-work balance. They'll just be another knackered key worker wanting a change of pace. There's a lot of us about, you know," she said. Lucy opened her mouth, but before she could reply, Jack appeared in front of the bar and loudly declared the pub quiz was about to start. He had changed into a ridiculous shiny gold jacket that was far too small for him.

"Ladies and gentlemen," he began in the dramatic game-show host voice he always put on for the quiz, "I'm pleased to announce that the theme for tonight's quiz is...Yorkshire!"

This was greeted with a loud cheer from the three elderly farmers who sat at the bar. They never joined in answering the questions but spent most of the evening heckling the host. They were quickly hushed by Shirley, who had left the kitchen and taken over the bar from her son. She was a large woman, with a ready smile, who changed the colour of her hair as often as her son changed the barrels of beer. Tonight, it was aubergine streaked with lilac.

"Okay question number one," said Jack. "What is the highest peak in Yorkshire? Question two…"

Lucy sipped her drink and glanced around the room while Rachel began scribbling down the answers. In the corner by the open fire, sat Reverend Davenport, Doctor Robertson, and Colonel Marsden, Caroline's bridge partner. They were the only ones who took the quiz seriously and always won. Opposite her, Ben, the local vet, had made up a team with Dan, one of Rachel's many cousins. They were joined by another dark-haired, attractive man. Lucy thought she recognised him from somewhere but couldn't place him. The three of them were far more interested in their pints than the questions. Over in the snug, Nora Parkin and her two cronies were huddled together like a coven. Guy was in there too, but she couldn't see who he was talking to. He caught her eye and gave her a friendly wave.

"AND NOW OUR last question," announced Jack in the same silly voice, half an hour later. "Which group had a hit in the 1990s with 'Common People'?"

"Yes, finally one I know," squealed Lucy gleefully grabbing hold of the pen.

"What's that got to do with Yorkshire?" asked Doctor Robertson indignantly.

"They were from Sheffield," replied Jack.

"South Yorkshire doesn't count," complained one of the hecklers, to more applause.

THE CHURCH CLOCK was striking eleven and Lucy and Rachel were the last to leave the pub. After the quiz and a supper of fish and chips, Jack had put an ABBA CD on. Then the three of them had danced around the snooker table, earning themselves more disapproving looks from Nora. Lucy didn't care. She threw her head back and laughed as Jack twirled her around, then lifted Rachel into the air. She was enjoying herself, having fun; something she hadn't done in a long time.

She waved goodbye to her two friends and as she walked home alone in the moonlight, she hummed and swayed to the tune of "Dancing Queen" that was still playing in her head. She swished her dress so the hem skimmed the long grass on the verge and then looked up at the star-filled sky as an owl screeched overhead. As she drifted past the avenue of old oak trees there was a loud crack. She froze and turned her head. There was a glint of pale light and a shadow disappeared between the trees. Lucy held her breath for a moment, then told herself she was being silly. It must have been a deer in the moonlight.

WHEN LUCY ARRIVED back at the Hall, she found Joan

yawning on the sofa while watching an old episode of *Antiques Roadshow.*

"Everything okay?" she asked shrugging off her jacket and ruffling the ears of Pickle, who had dashed over to greet her.

"Yes fine, love," replied the older lady, removing her glasses and rubbing her tired eyes. "Freddie went up at nine, good as gold. I've just been to check on him and he's fast asleep. Bill's emptying the buckets. The forecast said there'll be more rain tonight."

Lucy groaned as she flopped down on to the sofa. "We'll be swimming out of here by tomorrow."

Joan leaned over and gave her a hug. "I know it's none of my business, but couldn't you sell something—you know, a painting or a vase?" She pointed to the television screen. "Some of the things they show you on here go for ever such a lot of money."

"I wish I could—" Lucy sighed "—but apparently, I don't own anything on the estate. Everything is in Rupert's name; none of it belongs to me."

Joan paused for a moment as if she was trying to pick her next words carefully, then looked up as her husband entered the room, drying his hands on a towel.

"Well, you never know, Lady H," he said, "he might still come back. You can't give up hope."

Lucy stood up but couldn't bring herself to look at either of them. All the happiness she had felt in the pub seemed to have seeped out of her. "I won't," she said quietly.

Bill and Joan exchanged a look.

"Would you like us to stay the night?" asked Joan gently.

Lucy shook her head and managed a smile. "No thanks, I'll be fine, I promise." She hugged them both goodnight and watched as they walked arm in arm down the drive and back to the gatehouse. Part of her wished she was returning with them to their cosy home. They were like family to her, even if Bill did always insist on calling her Lady H.

She whistled for the dogs to come in after their last run in the grounds, then locked and bolted the back door. Slowly she made her way upstairs, flicking off light switches and checking doors and windows were secure as she went. Once she jumped in fright, but it was only her own reflection looking back at her from the dark glass. Her footsteps echoed after her as she walked down the long corridors. This nightly routine was the worst part of her day; the time she felt most alone, even with Freddie and the dogs. A house like Hartwell Hall was never meant to be lived in by just a mother and her little boy.

At the top of the stairs, she could see the door to Freddie's room was still open, his night light casting a warm glow out into the corridor.

Lucy crept inside and over to his bed. He looked so peaceful, snuggled under his dinosaur duvet clutching his favourite triceratops. Pickle pushed past her and leapt onto the bed, turning around twice before settling contentedly at Freddie's feet. Lucy leaned forward and brushed her son's forehead with her lips. He shifted slightly and opened his eyes.

"Mum, do you want to know what I wished for?" he whispered.

"Okay," replied Lucy quietly, then held her breath. Not

knowing what she would say if it was about Rupert.

"I wished dinosaurs would come back to life, you know like in that film." He turned over, so his back was now facing her. "But now I've told you, it won't come true. It was meant to be a secret."

Lucy felt a wave of relief wash over her. Gently, she stroked his sticking-up hair back down and kissed him on the top of his head.

"That's all right, my darling. Don't worry, I won't tell a soul. I'm very good at keeping secrets."

"Night, Mum," he whispered.

"Goodnight, Freddie. I love you."

She turned and tiptoed out of his room and pulled the door closed behind her. Her own room was a little further down the corridor and was dominated by a vast antique four-poster bed. She shivered as she slid in between the sheets. It was far too big and cold to sleep in alone. From the corridor there was a soft tapping sound, then her door creaked open. A second later a cold wet nose pushed against her bare arm.

"Come on up, old girl," whispered Lucy as the heavily pregnant Labrador clambered onto the bed. A few moments later she was snoring loudly, and Lucy couldn't help envying her. It would be hours before she fell asleep. Raindrops were beating against the window, but it wasn't the rain keeping her awake. All she could think about was why a detective from London wanted to rent a cottage in Hartwell.

Chapter Two

Rachel stretched out her leg and nudged the tap with her toe. Another trickle of hot water ran into the already full bathtub. Her fingertips were wrinkled like prunes, but she intended to wallow for a while longer. She lowered her shoulders a little further below the bubbles and sighed. Thank God it was Saturday, and she didn't have to work. Not that she didn't enjoy her job, at least most of the time, but it was good not to have to dash off. She tilted her head to the left, so she could see out of the tiny bathroom window. The sun was shining brightly down on the three apple trees blossoming in her garden and beyond the garden wall the moors stretched out as far as the eye could see. Wild and free and untamed. It would be the perfect day to saddle up Bailey and go for a ride. Perhaps she would get the chance, but even on a weekend her time wasn't always her own. As if to prove her point, her mobile phone began ringing from where it was charging in her bedroom. With another sigh, she leaned forward and pulled out the plug, then carefully stepped on to the tiled floor as the water slowly gurgled away.

Pulling her bathrobe on and with her long hair wrapped in a towel, she padded through into her bedroom. She was short enough not to need to duck under the low, crooked doorframe. Her phone had stopped ringing, but she picked it up and checked the screen. One missed call from Lucy. At one time, she would have called back immediately. Who was she kidding? At one time, she would have always had her phone to hand in case Lucy called. She'd looked amazing in that red dress last night and had been so happy to get a question right in the quiz. Jack, bless him, always threw in a pop music question for Lucy.

That was the thing about Luce, with her big blue eyes, long blonde hair, and slightly breathless voice, people always seemed to want to do things for her, help her, without her ever needing to ask.

A patchwork quilt made by her mother covered the brass-framed double bed. Rachel flopped down on to it and pressed play on the voicemail.

"Rach? It's me." The panic in Lucy's voice made Rachel sit up and hold her breath. "I'm having a bit of a nightmare. Tilly is having her puppies, right in the middle of my bed, would you believe? It's made a terrible mess. There's three so far, but the old girl's panting an awful lot. I've phoned Ben, but I don't know what else to do. Call when you can. Bye."

Rachel exhaled with relief and fought the urge to dash round to the hall immediately. She picked up one of the photos on her bedside table. It was of the two of them in Amsterdam, grinning for the camera as they sipped beer by the side of a canal. With her index finger, she gently stroked Lucy's face. Very slowly and painfully, she was managing to wean herself away from the woman, who could only ever be her best friend. Lockdown had been a blessing in disguise.

Not seeing Lucy for months on end had been both torture and Rachel's salvation. She was about to return her call, when the phone rang. It was Lucy again. With extreme self-control, Rachel let it go to voicemail once more and listened.

"Crisis over, Rach! Ben's here now and he's helped deliver the last puppy. Mummy and babies all doing well. I don't know who's the most excited: Freddie or Pickle! Speak soon."

Rachel leaned back and sighed. With Ben Bannister—the quiet but capable, tall Scottish vet—on site, at least she didn't need to feel guilty about not taking Lucy's call. She looked up at the huge map of the world hanging on the wall above her bed. When she'd bought it, the plan had been to add a pin for every place she visited. So far there were only three: Amsterdam, Paris, and Barcelona. All lovely places, but she longed to go somewhere that couldn't be booked as a city break from Leeds Bradford Airport. She wanted to immerse herself in other cultures, not just spend a few days sightseeing. Since coming home to Hartwell, she'd hardly been away, and she couldn't blame that on the pandemic entirely.

As her infatuation with Lucy grew, she'd wanted to stay as near to her as possible. Lucy had lived in the village for a few years, but they only became friends when Freddie started at the school. At the same time, Rachel's relationship with Charlotte, her girlfriend at university, had ended. The two of them planned to go travelling together, but in the end, Charlotte had got tired of waiting for Rachel to finish sorting out her family's problems. Now she lived in Sydney with her new girlfriend. Occasionally, when doing some late-night scrolling, Rachel would see Facebook posts of the two of them surfing or having dinner in some fancy harbourside restaurant.

All her life Rachel had been sensible, pragmatic, yet she'd spent the last few years torturing herself with the possibility things might change, that one day Lucy would feel more than friendship for her, but never daring to tell anyone her true feelings. She would swing from being filled with optimism when Lucy chose her as the first person to call in a crisis, only to descend into gloom as she watched someone like awful Guy Lovell flirting with her and making her laugh. Rupert had been the same—arrogant, pompous, condescending—but Lucy hadn't realised until it was too late. Then as their relationship began to disintegrate, she'd turned to Rachel.

"You're such an amazing friend, Rach!" she'd said a million times, but Rachel had always hoped for something more.

Outside the church clock was striking nine. With a groan, Rachel swung her feet off the bed. Sitting around daydreaming wouldn't do her any good. If she wanted to fit in a ride today, she would need to get a move on. A few minutes later, she was dressed in jodhpurs and a T-shirt and locking her front door. Her cottage was next door to the pub and she spotted Jack lumbering over to his little vintage sports car parked on the cobbles.

"Where are you off to so early?" she called out as she made her way over to him. Jack raised his hand and waved.

"Thirsk," he replied, slowly squeezing himself in behind the steering wheel. "I want to be first in the queue when the barbers open. I need to look my best if two single ladies are arriving in the village today."

Rachel frowned. "Do you mean Lucy's new tenants? I know the doctor is female; is the policer officer as well?"

"Yep." He grinned. "I'm pinning my hopes on her. You know I can't resist a woman in uniform."

"If she's a detective, she'll be plain clothes, Jack."

"Don't ruin my fantasies before she's even got here, Rach!"

"Sorry. How are you so well informed anyway? You know more about them than Lucy."

"Your uncle Frank told me when he delivered the milk this morning. Max had told him. He said there might be two new customers wanting to sign up for his round and no mention of husbands or boyfriends."

Rachel pulled a face at the mention of her brother-in-law. "If they do sign up, Max will probably charge Frank commission," she muttered.

Jack grinned as he slammed the door shut. "See you later, Rach."

With that he revved the engine and sped away. Rachel watched him go and shook her head. Jack's romantic history was one long list of disasters, but it never seemed to dent his enthusiasm. Maybe she could learn something from him.

She crossed the road and walked past the school and the church, up to the top of the hill, and through the familiar blue gates, noting that the paint was beginning to flake off. Church Farm was one of the few privately owned properties in the village and had been farmed by her family for generations. She made her way across the yard and couldn't help noticing the broken roof tile, the tractor still caked in mud, and the dripping tap. More signs that her father was no longer alive. When he had been in charge, everything was always maintained in pristine condition.

It was her father's accident that had led to Rachel returning home straight after finishing her teacher training. She remembered vividly that terrible phone call from her mother, telling her in a shaking voice that there had been an accident with the bailer, and the air ambulance had flown him to Leeds General Infirmary. The incredible doctors there had managed to save his life, but not his arm. Overnight Rachel's big, strong, cheerful, outgoing father became frightened, quiet, and withdrawn.

Back in the village, Rachel had been able to help with the accounts and support her parents through the long court case to gain compensation from the farm machinery manufacturers. The large payout had meant they could hire another farmhand and a shepherd to help run the farm, but they still relied on Rachel for so much. Then the job at the school had come up. Rachel had told herself it would only be for a year or two, but that had turned into four then five. She loved her students, well most of them, but teaching was meant to be something to help her see the world. She'd imagined teaching English to eager students in Africa, Asia, and South America. Now she wondered if she would ever leave the place where she'd been born.

The stone farmhouse was long and low like the White Hart and also like the pub, one of the village's oldest buildings. Rachel pushed open the back door that was always left unlocked and stepped into the kitchen. With its quarry-tiled floor, vast, well-scrubbed pine table, white Belfast sink, and old-fashioned range with the cat asleep on the pile of clean washing folded on top, it had barely changed since she was a child. When she arrived home from school there had always been a delicious smell of baking to greet her. Today, all she could smell was burning. There was no sign of her mother.

Rachel hurried over to the oven. The temperature dial was set far too high. She yanked open the door and was engulfed in a cloud of smoke. Stepping back coughing and blinking, she reached for the oven gloves. Then she pulled out the charred remains of what should have been an apple pie. Still coughing, she carried it over to the sink, placed it carefully down, and pushed the window open wide.

The noise had attracted the attention of Jenny, the elderly sheepdog. She came limping and woofing into the kitchen, then began wagging her tail furiously when she realised who it was. Rachel knelt down and stroked the old dog's ears as her mother finally appeared in the doorway.

"Hello, love. I didn't hear the door," she said, then spotting the smouldering pastry, "Oh dear, what happened?"

"You forgot about the pie again, Mum," replied Rachel, standing up to give her mother a hug. Mary Foxton was even smaller than Rachel, with wavy grey hair, soft brown eyes, and like her elder daughter, prone to putting on weight.

"Oh dear," she repeated, her face creasing in concern, "I only popped into the garden to sit in the sun for a few minutes. I didn't think it would be ready for another twenty minutes."

Rachel nodded. The garden was on the other side of the house. That explained why Jenny's keen nose hadn't alerted her mistress. Mary, who had once had total command of her kitchen, had started having several disasters lately. Rachel had managed to salvage a tray of jam tarts a couple of weeks ago and then one of the farm labourers, hearing Jenny barking, had rescued a burning chicken that Mary had forgotten about when she'd gone shopping.

"Never mind," said Rachel, giving her a reassuring smile, "you sit down, and I'll make us both a cup of tea."

She filled the heavy metal kettle and placed it on the hob, while Mary still shaking her head and looking confused, took a seat at the table. Rachel watched her carefully. She'd been like this since her husband had died. Perhaps it was to be expected; grief affected people in different ways, and it had been such a shock. They had all been so careful, nobody could understand how he'd caught Covid. He and Mary had isolated themselves, with Rachel dropping off groceries and prescriptions for them outside the back door, carefully disinfecting the bags and boxes before she left. They hadn't seen anyone for months, but still they had both succumbed, and her father, his body still weakened by the accident, hadn't been able to fight it.

What had made it worse was that due to the pandemic, none of them had been able to visit him in hospital to say goodbye. The man, so adored by his family and friends, had died alone. There was no wonder her mother was struggling, but still it was heart-breaking to watch. Rachel carried the two mugs of tea to the table and sat down next to her mother.

"So, Mum, how are you feeling? Are you sleeping any better?"

"I'm getting by, love. Dr. Robertson offered me some sleeping tablets, but I didn't fancy them."

Rachel nodded. She wasn't keen on the idea of her mother having sedatives either. She'd been so absent-minded recently she might easily take too many.

"Well, we have a new doctor arriving soon; perhaps she might be more helpful."

"Oh, Rachel, it isn't that Dr. Robertson isn't helpful," replied Mary causing Rachel to roll her eyes. The village doctor had been worse than useless when her father had been taken ill, but her mother wouldn't say a word against him and now wasn't the time to argue with her.

"If you say so, Mum. Look, I've been thinking, maybe a holiday would do you good. All the travel restrictions have been lifted now, almost everybody has been vaccinated and we could both do with a change of scene."

Mary shook her head and began nervously fiddling with her wedding ring.

"I'm not sure, love. There's such a lot to look after here."

"The lads would manage on their own for a week or so. Dan and Uncle Frank could keep an eye on things. I'd come with you and sort out all the arrangements. We could maybe go on a Mediterranean cruise. That would be relaxing," she suggested gently, but before her mother could answer, the back door opened and Becky, Rachel's younger sister, breezed in wearing a pink tracksuit, her bleached hair tied back in a high ponytail.

"Hi, Mum," she said brightly, then her face fell when she saw Rachel, "Oh you're here."

"Hello there, Becky love," said Mary with a smile. "Well

this is nice, having you both here at the same time. I haven't seen you for a while."

"I know, Mum, but I've been really busy," replied Becky, shooing away Jenny, who was moulting. Rachel raised an eyebrow. Her sister didn't work and employed a cleaner to take care of the four-bedroomed barn conversion she and Max rented from the estate. As far as Rachel could tell, all she'd been busy with was topping up her fake tan and getting her nails done.

It had been the same during the pandemic. She hadn't lifted a finger to help with her parents. When Rachel, worried because she had a slight temperature, had asked Becky to do the grocery shopping one week, her sister had told her bluntly, "I can't. Unlike you I have my own family to look after."

"How's that lovely granddaughter of mine?" asked Mary.

"Oh, Araminta is doing brilliantly," trilled Becky. "She's preparing for her first ballet exam and her tennis coach says she's a natural."

"That's wonderful," replied Mary, beaming, "and it reminds me, I bought her a teddy dressed as a ballerina last time I was in Thirsk. I'll just go and find it."

Rachel remained silent as her mother left the kitchen. She knew full well it was Mary paying for both the ballet and the tennis lessons. Becky had always been a social climber and was now pinning all her aspirations on to her four-year-old daughter. Max was even worse. He'd grown up in a modern semi in the suburbs of Manchester but was desperately trying to reinvent himself as a member of the landed gentry. When Rupert had been around, it had been almost comical to watch him try and copy the way his employer dressed and acted. Max would never understand that cufflinks bought from John Lewis would never be the same as ones inherited from your grandfather. As for his accent, it was painful to listen to him attempting to change his flat northern vowels into a clipped upper-class drawl.

"What have you got there?" she asked as she watched Becky casually place a bundle of brochures she'd been carrying down on the pine dresser.

"Just some things for Mum to look at when she has time," replied Becky in such a nonchalant way that Rachel was immediately suspicious. She stood up and walked over to take a look for herself. They all seemed to be about holiday cottages and for a second, she thought she'd misjudged her sister and she was here to encourage their mother to have a break too. However, upon closer inspection, she realised they were about building and renting out cottages.

"Are you and Max thinking about going into the tourism business?" she asked. Becky laughed her brittle, affected laugh that always set Rachel's nerves on edge.

"Oh no, not at our place, but Max had this brilliant idea of turning the stables here into a holiday cottage. He's worked out all the figures."

Rachel pursed her lips. Ever since, her father had received his compensation, her sister and brother-in-law had been finding ways for them to spend it.

"I don't think Mum's up to taking on that amount of work and having strangers staying here," she said, handing the brochures back to her sister.

"We'd take care of everything for her," said Becky with a

bright smile.

I bet you would, thought Rachel but instead she said, "And you seem to be forgetting the stables are occupied. Bailey lives there. You do remember my horse, Bailey?"

"Actually, Max was looking into it and it's not really fair. If you were to pay livery it would cost you a packet, but you stable him here for free and as Dad paid for him, then technically he's not yours..."

This was the last straw for Rachel. She drew herself up to her full height and jabbed a finger at Becky, who immediately recoiled.

"Dad bought Bailey and gave him to me as a gift. If either you or your husband so much as lay a finger on my horse, I'll swing for you both. Tell Mum I'll see her later."

Rachel stomped out of the house, before Becky could say anything else. She was so angry with her spoilt, selfish sister, that if she stayed, she wouldn't be able to stop herself slapping that smug little face. It had been the same since they were little. Rachel always the feisty one, sticking up for herself, while Becky whined, pouted, and sulked to get what she wanted. Sometimes she wished they were still children and she could pull Becky's hair to shut her up.

She marched over to the stables, where good old Bailey was munching hay, unaware that he'd been the cause of yet another argument between the two sisters. He looked up and whinnied a greeting when he heard Rachel slide back the bolt on his door. She stepped into the cool stable and rested her face on his soft brown neck, inhaling his sweet scent while she calmed down. For as long as she could remember, the stables had been her sanctuary, the place she came to when she felt the world was against her and she'd be damned if she was going to let anyone change that.

A few moments later, Bailey was saddled up and he and Rachel were trotting out of the yard and up the road to the open countryside. She closed her eyes for a second and breathed in the fresh air. This was exactly what she needed. The wind in her face, the sun on her back and a long ride across the moors to forget all about Becky, Max, and even Lucinda.

CHAPTER THREE

M EERA RAN HER finger along the shelves, checking she hadn't made a mistake. No, all was perfectly in order. Starting with Austen, then Brontë, right down to Thackeray on the bottom shelf. Now she had unpacked her beloved books, the cottage was beginning to feel like home. The first home that was truly hers. She had lived in Bradford with her parents, until her marriage, then she'd moved a few miles away to the modern detached house in Shipley, which Dev's parents had bought for them. The cottage was tiny in comparison, but soon as she'd seen the picture on the agent's website of the low-beamed ceilings and the shelves taking up an entire wall of the sitting room, she'd known this was the perfect place for her and Krish. At the thought of her son, she stopped and listened. There wasn't a sound coming from the first floor, so she quietly crept up the stairs.

Krish had insisted he wanted to unpack and arrange everything in his new bedroom himself; however, when Meera gently pushed open the door, she found only one box had been opened. Instead of unpacking, Krish was lying across his unmade bed on his stomach, with his binoculars trained on the fields and woods outside the window. Meera tiptoed over.

"What do you have to report?" she asked, quietly sitting down next to him. Krish shifted slightly but didn't lower his binoculars.

"Loads. I've lost count of how many rabbits I've seen and there was a squirrel, only a grey one though, of course. I heard a woodpecker, but I haven't seen him yet, and there was a buzzard circling for a while but then lots of rooks flew out of those woods and started mobbing him. Do you know what the collective name is for a group of rooks, Mum?"

"No, I don't," replied Meera, smiling indulgently. He was so enthusiastic. He'd barely paused for breath.

"It's a parliament. Isn't that cool? Not as cool as a group of crows though; they are called a murder."

"I don't think that's a very nice name," said Meera with a little shudder. She noticed his wildlife journal open on the floor. His observations had been jotted down in his tiny, but neat handwriting.

"Time for lunch," she declared. "What would you like?"

"Fish fingers?" asked Krish hopefully.

"Fish fingers coming up, but with salad not chips," said Meera pleased that she had got up early to go to the supermarket before they left that morning. She might not have unpacked all her pots and pans yet, but at least the fridge and freezer were full of Krish's favourites. She smiled ruefully to herself as she made her way back downstairs. No doubt her mother would be disappointed with her grandson's choice of meal. All those hours she had spent teaching Meera how to make the perfect saag aloo and all Krish ever wanted was pizza or fish fingers.

Oh well, it would just have to be added to the list of her

mother and father's other current disappointments. Top of that list was the fact that she and Krish had moved to North Yorkshire and that Dev would not be joining them. She paused next to one of the open boxes. Lying on top was their wedding photo. Dev looked so handsome in his brocade suit. He was grinning broadly for the camera, and she was standing by his side, smiling shyly, draped in red and gold. She shook her head. All those astrologers Dev's mother had consulted before the lavish ceremony certainly hadn't predicted how things would turn out. She'd never worn red again since that day. It would have felt like a bad joke. She picked up the photograph, slid it into an open drawer in the sideboard then pushed it closed with a satisfying thud. Really, she should never have bothered to pack it.

The sudden bleeping of her phone made her jump. Then she relaxed. Only her parents had her new number, and they were under strict instructions not to give to anyone else. After her last telephone conversation with her husband, if Dev wanted to contact her, he could email. She checked the text. It was from her mother.

Your father says it's not too late to change your mind. XX

Meera's heart sank. Since announcing she and Krish were moving away, her father had refused to speak to her. Her mother had tried to act as peacemaker, but she didn't understand her daughter's decision either.

"We haven't seen you for months and now we have finished shielding, you are moving away," she'd wailed. Meera had attempted to explain why she needed to go, in a way that wouldn't shock them. She told them working seven days a week, through a pandemic that had affected her own community so brutally, had left her exhausted. This was true, but it wasn't the only reason she needed a fresh start. Her adored father, who had worked so hard to create a new life for them here, simply couldn't understand why his dutiful daughter would suddenly do something so out of character. Looking both angry and hurt, the last thing he'd said to her was: "Marriage vows are for life. A wife should be with her husband."

Dev hadn't helped of course. When her parents had confronted him about what was going on, he'd smiled his charming smile and told them it was nothing. He'd trotted out platitude after platitude.

"This will soon blow over. It's just a storm in a teacup. She'll soon come around."

Meera shook her head. She was used to him lying to her, but she couldn't forgive him being dishonest to her parents. The man was a total coward. Not feeling up to replying to her mother's text, she went to open the freezer door, but stopped when she heard an unfamiliar clip-clopping sound.

"Mum, look there's a horse outside," Krish called down in excitement.

Meera went to the window to take a look. Krish was so thrilled by every little thing their new home had to offer. She peered out and gasped. The sound of the brown pony might have been unfamiliar, but she recognised his rider immediately. She dashed to the front door and pulled it open.

"Rachel!" she called out.

The rider turned to look at her in surprise, then her face broke into a smile of recognition. She pulled her horse to a halt and jumped down.

"Meera Patel! Oh my God, it is you. I haven't seen you in years." She rushed over and hugged Meera. "Are you the new doctor?"

"Yes, a Kumar now, not a Patel." Meera laughed when Rachel finally released her. "I remembered how pretty Hartwell looked in all the photos you had on your wall at uni, so when the chance to work here came up, I couldn't resist. I never imagined you would still be here though. I thought you'd be off in some exotic location."

Rachel's smile faded a little as she shrugged. "Oh, you know how it can be with families," she said.

Meera nodded, she certainly did. Her parents had been happy for her to study medicine at Leeds University, but had insisted she live at home rather than in halls and had refused to let her go to any of the social events the other students enjoyed. Rachel had been one of the few friends she'd made there. The two girls had met at one of the university book clubs, the only extracurricular activity Meera's parents had deemed acceptable. She remembered Rachel leaving abruptly in her final year, only returning briefly to sit her exams. Meera had stayed on for another two years of study and over time they had lost touch.

"Can I stroke the horse please, Mum," said Krish, who had appeared beside her.

"This is my son Krish. Krish, this is Rachel Foxton, an old friend of mine."

Krish smiled shyly as Rachel held out her hand.

"It's nice to meet you Krish. You can sit on Bailey if you like. He's very calm."

Krish's face lit up, but Meera shook her head.

"Thank you, Rachel, that is a kind offer, but Krish has allergies. He hasn't been near a horse before. I don't know how he would react. Perhaps you'd like to come in for a cup of tea if you can…what do you call it? Park? Bailey there."

Rachel smiled but took a step back. "I'd love to, but I'd better not. I'm covered in horsehair. I'd hate to make Krish ill. We'll catch up soon though and, Krish, I look forward to seeing you at school."

With that she remounted Bailey and gave them a cheery wave as she trotted away.

"What did she mean, Mum?" asked Krish.

"I think Rachel, or Miss Foxton as you should call her now, might be your new teacher."

"That's so cool! Do you think she rides the horse to school?"

THAT NIGHT, AS it began to grow dark, Meera checked that both the front and back door were locked, and the windows were secure. A car pulled up at the cottage next door. Rap music blaring from its stereo. Meera frowned as she peered out of the window. She hoped her new neighbours didn't have noisy teenagers living at home. She heard the car door, then the front door slam, then silence. With a feeling of relief, she began her night-time routine of ensuring all plug sockets and lights were turned off.

Upstairs she found Krish still awake and reading a book about birds in bed. His bedroom window was wide open. When his mother moved to close it, he immediately protested. "Please can we leave it open, Mum? I'm listening out for owl calls. I've heard a tawny but not a barn yet."

"What's the difference?" asked Meera as she peered out of the window. There was no way to get there except from across the fields and no ladders close at hand or trees near enough to climb.

"The tawny does the twit-twoo and the barn is more of a screecher. Please, Mum. The fresh air is really helping with my breathing."

Meera shook her head ruefully and lowered the window a few inches. "You should be a lawyer coming up with all these arguments." She stopped herself saying, 'like your father'. "I'll half close it okay? Now take your inhaler before you go to sleep."

Krish obediently removed his brown inhaler from the drawer in his bedside table and took two puffs before Meera kissed him goodnight.

Then she went next door to her own room and changed into her favourite silk nightdress embroidered with cherry blossom. She climbed into bed and lay there listening. Apart from the occasional screech that she now knew was a barn owl out hunting, there was nothing. There had been no need to worry about her new neighbours. No traffic, no banging doors, no shouting, and best of all no rasped breathing from her son's room. Krish hadn't needed his blue, emergency inhaler once today. Then to top everything off, she'd found her old friend.

The move to Hartwell had definitely been the right decision. If only she could make her parents see that too.

CHAPTER FOUR

J O SLAPPED HER hand against the horn impatiently. The drive up from London had taken forever and now she was held up yet again. She'd been stuck behind this tractor for ten minutes and these stupid, twisty roads were too narrow to overtake on. Finally, the great lumbering machine turned off into a field, without bothering to indicate of course. Jo slammed her foot down on the accelerator and turned up the volume on the car stereo. The angry tones of the latest grime star filled her ears. The music matched her mood.

Since turning off the A1, she had seen more sheep than people. Sure, the fields and hills were pretty, but there was nothing here. No takeaways, supermarkets, gyms, or clubs. This must be what purgatory was like. She remembered Sister Gertrude, who was in charge of the fourth orphanage she'd been put in, explaining in great detail the place of suffering where sinners had to be cleansed of their sins before entering heaven. She clearly thought Jo would be spending a lot of time there. Well, she'd been right. Now she was going to have to find a way to redeem herself if she was ever going to get back to the Met, never mind make inspector.

It was so late that it was almost dark when the annoying voice of her sat nav told her that she had reached her destination. Sure enough there was the sign for Lilac Cottage hanging above the cream door. She pulled over on to the cobbles and switched off the engine. She hauled her holdall out the boot and slung it over her shoulder, thankful that she made a point of never owning more than she could fit into one bag. At least it wouldn't take long to unpack. Max Foxton-Smith, the smarmy agent, with the weird accent had told her the key to the cottage would be left under a plant pot at the front door. When she'd queried how secure that was, he'd actually laughed at her down the phone. Patronising sod! But it had confirmed her fears: crime wasn't going to be much of an issue here.

She retrieved the key, unlocked the door, flicked on a light, and stepped inside. The cottage was what estate agents called quaint with low-beamed ceilings, sash windows, and uneven floors. More importantly it was furnished. There was a sofa and TV in the sitting room, table and chairs in the kitchen, and a bed and wardrobe upstairs. However, the bed hadn't been made up and Jo couldn't be arsed to do it now. After a quick rummage through her bag, she found her toothbrush and toothpaste. She splashed some water on her face and stared at the mirror for a second. Two green eyes stared back at her. They were her only distinguishing feature. Average height, average build, with light brown hair she wore tied back, and occasionally trimmed herself with nail scissors. Her eyes were the only thing that made her stand out from the crowd and right now they had bags under them as big as her holdall.

With a sigh, she went back downstairs. She was still wearing her vest top and cargo pants but pulled off her trainers. Flopping down on the sofa, she pulled her leather jacket over her, closed her eyes, and tried to get to sleep in the deafening silence.

RAT-A-TAT-TAT! RAT-A-TAT-TAT! SOMEONE was knocking loudly on her neighbour's door. Jo groaned. She'd only just managed to get back to sleep again after the bloody church bells had woken her up. Had nobody heard of a Sunday lie-in around here? Reluctantly, she unfolded herself from the sofa and went to investigate. She stood at the edge of the window and carefully pulled back the net curtain half an inch. A tall, blonde woman with one of those loud, posh voices that carried was talking to the petite dark-haired woman who lived next door. Then to her horror the blonde turned and walked the few steps over the cobbles to her door.

Jo dropped the curtain, but she was too late. The blonde had spotted her and was now smiling and waving. A second later there was another cheerful rat-a-tat-tat, this time at her door. Jo swore under her breath. She'd have to answer it now. With a heavy sigh she pulled open the door and assessed her visitor. She was wearing a floral dress with a denim jacket and had the air of natural confidence that the upper classes all seemed to inherit along with their titles and houses. She thrust a bunch of flowers towards Jo.

"Hello, you must be Detective Sergeant Ormond. I'm Lucy Hanley. I thought I'd drop by and welcome you to Hartwell."

"Thanks," mumbled Jo reluctantly taking the flowers. What the hell was she meant to do with these?

"So do you plan on staying here long?" asked Lucy.

Jo frowned. "Hanley did you say? That's the name of the person I'm renting from."

"Yes, that's me, or rather the estate."

"Then surely you know I've taken the cottage for six months."

Lucy looked embarrassed as she tucked her hair behind her ear. "Well, yes, I do I suppose. It was more that I was wondering if you were here for work or taking an extended break. I hear a lot of you key workers need to recharge your batteries, so to speak. I thought you might be using this place as a sort of bolthole for weekends or something."

"I'm here for work," Jo replied.

Lucy clearly had no idea what a police sergeant earned if she thought they could afford to live in London and have a bolthole in the country.

"Oh right," she began chewing her lower lip. "Well, I've just invited your neighbour, our new doctor, to come along to the village hall tonight. There's a parish council meeting at six, which will be awfully dull, but it's a chance to meet everyone or mostly everyone, so I thought maybe you'd like to join us too."

"Maybe," replied Jo, thinking there was nothing she would like to do less. There followed an uncomfortable few seconds when Lucy looked like she was expecting Jo to say more. When it became clear she wasn't going to, her face fell and she finally stepped back.

"Well nice to meet you. I hope you'll be very happy

here," she said.

"Thanks," said Jo and shut the door. This is what she'd been afraid of. All the village busybodies knocking on her door every two minutes. Dumping the flowers on the table, she retrieved her jacket from the sofa and began rummaging through the pockets. She needed a cigarette. Glancing up at the ceiling, she swore again as she noticed the smoke alarm. She'd been so pissed off when she was looking for somewhere to live, she'd forgotten to check and now she'd ended up in a 'no smoking' rental.

After unlocking the back door, she stepped out into a small cottage garden. Two slightly rickety chairs were placed on the square patio area, then there was a lawn, and a large tree with purple blooms. Jo knew nothing about flowers or plants, but she guessed this must be the lilac tree the cottage was named after. She sat on one chair, put her feet up on the other and lit her cigarette. Tilting her face to the sun, she inhaled deeply. A few moments later she heard a small cough and a voice call out, "Hello there! Excuse me!"

Jo opened her eyes and saw her neighbour, with her sleek dark bob and large brown eyes peering over the wall.

"Hello, I'm Meera Kumar," she said. "I'm sorry to bother you, but could I ask you not to smoke? You see my son has asthma and I understood both these properties were non-smoking. I am sorry."

"No need to keep apologising," said Jo, standing up and dropping her cigarette on to the patio. "You're right. I was in breach of the rental agreement. I'm Jo."

She jumped up on her chair and briefly grasped her new neighbour's hand. Then just as quickly, she jumped down and went inside, before Meera could ask anything else of her. Perhaps it was time to explore her new surroundings. She was beginning to get cabin fever, and she could kill for a coffee. After grabbing her jacket, phone, and wallet she stepped out of her front door and on to the cobbles where she'd parked her car. Slipping on her sunglasses, she walked along the stream to the end of the lane. She turned on to what seemed to be the main street and began walking up the path towards the village shop she remembered passing the night before.

The church bells were ringing again and smartly dressed people began drifting out of the heavy wooden gates that led to the graveyard. Jo managed to mumble a few hellos in response to their cheery "good mornings." How did people get anything done around here if they kept stopping to chat to everyone?

She pushed open the door of the village shop and a bell jangled to announce her arrival. The woman behind the counter with a pinched face and a tight perm looked her up and down as she entered. Jo picked up a basket and edged her way down the first of the two narrow aisles. The range of goods was limited and not very appealing. She only grabbed what she deemed essential—coffee, beer, bread, and several large bags of crisps—then dumped her basket on the counter. The sour-faced woman started to tap the prices into the large, old-fashioned cash register in front of her.

"I'll have two packets of Marlboros, as well please," Jo said.

"So, which one are you then, the doctor or the police-woman?" the sour face asked, adding the cigarettes to her pile of goods.

"I'm a police officer," replied Jo, stressing the last word. What century was this woman living in?

"You here about his lordship?"

"Who?"

"Lord Rupert Hanley. He disappeared before the first lockdown. Nobody has seen hide nor hair of him since that night's parish council meeting."

Jo shook her head. "Never heard of him."

The woman looked disappointed by this news. "The police haven't come up with anything all this time. There are those that say they won't, and that it's all down to the old Druid's curse."

"Yeh?" replied Jo, unimpressed. She didn't believe in curses or ghosts. In her experience, humans were cruel, selfish, greedy, and violent. They were more than capable of causing pain and misery without any assistance from evil spirits.

"There are others that say that wife of his knows more that she's letting on."

Jo raised an eyebrow, surely she didn't mean the dizzy blonde who had turned up on her doorstep. She hardly seemed the vengeful wife type, but then maybe she wasn't simply paying a social call. After all she had wanted to know what Jo was doing in the village as well; only she'd been a bit more subtle about it.

Jo paid and picked up her carrier bag, then stepped outside before the owner could pour any more poison into her ear. She glanced across the road and noticed that the pub was now open. The delicious smell of roast beef wafting across reminded her that she hadn't eaten anything since stopping on the motorway for a burger. She decided to skip breakfast and go straight to lunch.

"Hello, hello, hello," said the bearlike man behind the bar. He had a broad grin and a crooked nose.

Jo scowled. "Are you trying to be funny?"

His face fell. "No, friendly. I'm Jack; I'm the landlord here. Welcome to the White Hart."

He thrust his hand out across the bar towards her and reluctantly she took it.

"Jo. Do you actually serve customers or just annoy them?"

"What would you like?" he asked, his grin returning.

"I'll have a bottle of Stella. Cheers."

"We've got some nice pale ales on draught."

"And if I wanted bitter, I would have asked for it," replied Jo. Honestly what was wrong with him? Did he think that because she was a woman, she didn't know what she wanted to drink?

"You'll find it a lot cheaper to have a drink up here instead of down in that London," said one of the several old, flat-cap-wearing men at the bar.

"How do you know I'm from London?" she asked. The other flat caps started laughing and Jack grinned too.

"The accent sort of gives it away. Plus, we've all heard the news that a sergeant from the Met is moving into the village." He leaned forward and lowered his voice. "By the way I love your accent."

Jo scowled again and shifted uncomfortably on the bar stool. She'd spent most of her life being anonymous. A nameless face in a big city. It felt weird having strangers know who she was.

"Now what can I tempt you with from the menu."

"If I order something, will you promise to drop the cheery banter?"

Jack looked as if he were seriously considering her suggestion. "If you order the roast beef, I promise to leave you in peace for at least ten minutes."

"Okay, but no Yorkshire puddings?"

There was a sharp intake of breath from all the men at the bar.

"I'm sorry, but I don't like them," she said with a shrug.

"They probably don't make them properly down south," said Jack. "I promise you'll like ours."

"Fine," said Jo, her mouth twitching into a smile despite herself. "Now I'm going to take my beer and find a nice quiet table."

"I'll bring your food over," he called after her.

Jo found a table in the corner as far away from the bar as possible. She took her phone out of her pocket and began googling Lord Rupert Hanley. Under normal circumstances, the disappearance of a member of the aristocracy would have been front-page news, but March that year had been anything but normal. Everyone was obsessed with face masks, transmission rates, and whether there were enough toilet rolls in the supermarkets, to care if some lord had gone AWOL.

She managed to find a couple of reports, both accompanied by pictures of a good-looking man with blue eyes and light brown hair. Apparently, he was last seen at a meeting of the parish council, the night the first lockdown was announced. He'd left with the other council members and was thought to have walked home to Hartwell Hall, but had never arrived. His wife of nine years, Lady Lucinda Hanley, had reported him missing the next day. Police had appealed for information, saying that it was possible he was in London. This struck Jo as strange. Why would they think he wouldn't be spending lockdown with his family?

Jo looked up from her phone and glared. The bleached blonde woman at the next table had a really annoying giggle. Jo didn't like gigglers. In her book, giggling was one step away from simpering. It reminded her of her school days. She'd been to loads of schools, but every one had a similar clique of girls, who thought they were cool and found it hilarious that Jo lived in a children's home and had no idea who her parents were.

"Oh, you are funny, Max!"

God, there she went again. Someone should tell her to lay off the sunbed too—she was turning orange. At that moment, Jack appeared with her food.

"Excellent as always, Jack. My compliments to the chef," called out the man with the giggler. Jo frowned. She knew that fake-posh voice. It was the agent she'd rented the cottage from.

"Cheers, Max, I'll let Mum know," replied Jack, placing Jo's plate in front of her. "By the way, have you two met..." Jo caught his eye and gave her head a little shake. The last thing she wanted was to start a conversation with the agent and giggle girl. Jack smiled at her and cleared his throat. "Have you two managed to look at the dessert menu?" he said instead.

"I really shouldn't. I'm watching my figure, Jack!" Accompanied by yet another giggle.

"Nonsense, there isn't an ounce of fat on you, Becky," replied Jack as he walked, slightly limping, back to the bar. "You're like Hartwell's own Cara Delevingne."

Jo shook her head. Talk about having the gift of the gab. She devoured her lunch. Annoyingly the gobby landlord had been right about the Yorkshire pudding. Not wanting to hang around, she went up to the bar to pay. There was a young woman with long dark hair, wearing jodhpurs and T-shirt, chatting to Jack as she ate her lunch. Jo handed over her money without a word.

"Thanks, lovely. Does this mean the White Hart has a new regular?" Jack asked eagerly.

"Unless there's another pub in walking distance," muttered Jo.

"Excellent! Now, you just need to tell me what time I should pick you up tonight. I thought I could show you what Thirsk has to offer," said Jack as he made his way to the back of the bar to get her change.

"Is he for real?" asked Jo incredulously, turning to her neighbour.

"You've made quite an impression," replied the woman with dark hair, as she speared a piece of carrot.

"You mean he isn't like this with everyone?" asked Jo.

The woman shook her head. There was another loud peal of giggles.

"Jesus, she should be gagged," groaned Jo.

"Tell me about it. She's my sister," said her neighbour.

"Christ, sorry," apologised Jo.

The other woman smiled and held out her hand. "Don't

be. Why do you think I'm sat over here? I'm Rachel by the way."

"So, what do you think?" asked Jack.

Jo took her change. "Sorry, I've already got a date with the parish council. See you around."

LATER THAT AFTERNOON, following her huge lunch and a snooze, Jo was sprawled out on the sofa, a tube of Pringles resting on her chest as she flicked through the TV channels. There was nothing worth watching and thanks to the useless broadband here, she couldn't connect to Netflix. She needed something to distract her. All she could think about was the reason she'd found herself stuck here, in the middle of nowhere. It had been her own stupid fault.

Her team had been investigating Roy Sutcliffe and his gang for months. He and his associates were responsible for trafficking about half of all the cocaine that came into the capital. Jo and the rest of her team had spent months going through bank accounts and phone records. Not to mention the endless hours sitting in the back of a cramped surveillance van, taking photos of anyone or anything that might be connected to him.

The briefing before they went out had been tense. Palmer, the new inspector, who seemed to have taken an instant dislike to Jo, had stated bluntly that she wanted no cock-ups. She'd also reminded them that due to Covid regulations they should be wearing face coverings. Jo was convinced this was the reason for her mistake. As usual she removed the warrant card on the lanyard around her neck while she put on her stab vest, then she'd grabbed her face mask, but forgotten the lanyard.

The deal hadn't gone according to plan. Sutcliffe must have sensed something was wrong and made a run for it. Jo was the one to chase him down and arrest him, but as soon as she read him his rights and cuffed him, she realised her mistake. So did Sutcliffe. To make matters worse, they didn't find any weapons or drugs on him. Within minutes of his slick, smooth-talking lawyer arriving at the station, they'd had to release him. She would never forget the smug look on Sutcliffe's face.

"Dear oh dear, a plain-clothes copper trying to arrest someone without their warrant card. Better luck next time, eh darling."

Palmer had given her a choice: demotion or a transfer. Jo couldn't bear the thought of losing the rank she'd worked so hard for, so she chose a transfer. She'd expected a sideways move, maybe to vice or at the absolute worst traffic, not to be shifted over two hundred miles north, to a force with one of the lowest crime rates in the country.

What had hurt even more was that none of her team had spoken up for her. She knew they were angry with her and worried for the own careers. The new inspector had made it clear she wanted to make changes, but not one of the five guys she'd worked with for over two years had supported her. Not even, Paul, who she'd hooked up with when she was either bored or drunk. She checked her phone for about the tenth time that day. No, not one text or message to ask her how the move went or to wish her well. It looked like she was on her own as usual.

"Two-faced bastards," she muttered under her breath.

From outside there was the sudden sound of voices, then there was a knock at the door. She glanced at her watch and groaned. It was six o'clock.

"Hello again," said Lucy brightly, as Jo opened the door. Next to her stood the small dark-haired woman from next door. "This is Meera Kumar. Meera, this is Jo."

"We've already met," replied Jo and noticed her neighbour had changed out of the tracksuit bottoms and T-shirt she had been wearing earlier into a smart orange shift dress and low heels. With a sigh, Jo brushed the crisp crumbs off her face and T-shirt and grabbed her jacket.

The three of them arrived at the village to find the place heaving. Rachel waved them over.

"I've saved you some seats," she said. "It feels like half of Hartwell has come out to meet you two."

Jo slumped silently into her seat, not making eye contact with anyone. The woman from the shop was patrolling the rows of seats, ensuring nobody had more than one biscuit with their plastic cup of tea.

"Nora takes her role as the secretary of the parish council very seriously," whispered Lucy to Jo and Meera.

"Is the face mask really necessary, Nora? It doesn't make you look very welcoming," asked Rachel, loudly.

"Yes, it is," Nora snapped back. "Relaxing restrictions too early is how it kept spreading before. As soon as the first lockdown was lifted the village was swamped by day trippers from Leeds and Bradford and God knows where else. It's a pity we didn't have a moat or a wall."

"But practically everyone has been vaccinated," argued Rachel.

"That may be true, but we all know some communities have been slower than others to get protected," she said staring pointedly at Meera, "and some of us here might still be vulnerable."

Lucy raised her eyebrows. "Crikey," she murmured, "I can't think of anyone less vulnerable than Nora." Rachel grunted in agreement while Meera politely pretended not to hear and continued to smile at the other villagers. Max appeared and pushed his way past them to try and get to a seat near the front. He'd changed his clothes since lunchtime and was now wearing hideous red trousers and a checked shirt with a cord tie. Rachel rolled her eyes as soon as she saw her brother-in-law.

"What a state," she tutted. "It looks like he's been taking style tips from Guy."

"Who's Guy?" asked Jo, interested despite herself.

"Our local MP," explained Rachel nodding towards a man with thick grey hair swept back from his round face, who was indeed wearing red trousers too. He was sat at a large oak table on the raised platform at the far end of the hall with what Jo assumed were the other members of the parish council. None of them looked like they would ever see sixty again.

"Oh gosh, Caroline is here," said Lucy suddenly. "I'd better go and say 'hello' or I'll be in trouble for ignoring her."

Jo gave Rachel a questioning look.

"Lucy's mother-in-law stroke dragon," replied Rachel. Jo

watched as Lucy hurried over to an elegant but stern-looking woman sitting at the oak table.

"Hello, Caroline, I didn't expect to see you here," said Lucy, bending down to kiss the older woman's well-powdered cheek.

"Why ever not? As a prominent member of the parish council and representative of the estate it's only right I should be here to welcome our new arrivals," she replied. "I had assumed you would be too busy caring for Freddie to attend. Speaking of which, I thought he could come for tea on Wednesday. Does that suit?"

"Hold on, I'll check his after-school activities," replied Lucy, looking flustered at being put on the spot. She dumped her bag on the table and began emptying the contents until she finally found the crumpled timetable Freddie had brought home. She quickly unfolded it accompanied by an impatient tut from Caroline. "Oh yes, Wednesday is fine. Thank you, Caroline. I'm sure Freddie will look forward to it," she said scribbling on the back of the timetable and smiling gratefully at Guy as he helped her put everything back in her bag, before she hurried back to her seat. Jo smiled to herself. Dragon was an understatement.

A tall elderly man rose to his feet and introduced himself as Colonel Marsden, chair of the parish council. He then introduced the other members and the meeting began. The first item on the agenda was agreeing the minutes of the last meeting, which had been held via Zoom. Then there was a lengthy discussion about whether to ask the county council to provide a new rubbish bin by the duck pond or whether the parish should fund it themselves. Jo closed her eyes and wondered if anyone would notice if she fell asleep. The colonel then invited Meera to say a few words. Jo watched as her new neighbour stepped confidently onto the platform and gave a concise and polished speech, introducing herself, thanking Dr. Robertson and telling the audience how happy she was to be in Hartwell. She sat down to enthusiastic clapping and Colonel Marsden rose to his feet again.

"Thank you very much, Dr. Kumar. I think I can speak for everyone when I say how happy we are to have you here," he said. "Next I'd like to welcome Detective Sergeant Jo Ormond."

All eyes turned to Jo. Her heart sank. She hated speaking in public.

"Almond like the nut?" asked Reverend Davenport, who seemed to be slightly deaf.

"No Ormond, like the hospital," replied Jo.

"How very unusual. And what is Jo short for? Is it Jo-anne or Josephine?" enquired Caroline.

"Just Jo."

"Perhaps you could give us some advice about protecting ourselves and our property?" suggested the colonel with an encouraging smile. Jo stood up and reluctantly took the spot recently vacated by Meera. With her hands still jammed in her pockets, she decided to treat this like a case briefing and imagine she was talking to the guys at work.

"Okay, well first up, protecting your property. Insurance companies will always insist on installing alarms, but in my experience the best deterrent against burglars is decent lighting, gravel around your house, and a dog with a really loud bark. That's a career burglar I'm talking about, someone who knows what he's doing. He's after a soft target, so make sure that isn't you. Needless to say, if it's some passing druggie trying to break in, they'll probably be high, so they won't be thinking straight. They take stupid risks. The bad news is they are more difficult to deter, but the good news is they are easier to catch."

She paused. Her audience were sitting in stunned silence. Jo noticed Meera was staring at the floor and both Rachel and Lucy were covering their mouths with their hands. Colonel Marsden cleared his throat loudly.

"Ah, well, yes, thank you, Sergeant Ormond. That sounds very useful. Those puppies of Tilly's will be in demand now I daresay, Lucy. Anything else?" he asked sounding a little wary.

"Well, I always keep a baseball bat next to the bed," replied Jo.

"A baseball bat?" echoed Reverend Davenport adjusting his glasses and looking like a startled owl. Jo shrugged, then noticed the row of cricket trophies to her left.

"Or a cricket bat would do, if that's more your sort of thing, but remember the law only allows for reasonable force when attacking an intruder, even in self-defence. Anything more than GBH and you could find yourself up in court. And nobody wants to go down for smacking a crackhead."

Nora gasped, her mouth full of biscuit behind the mask and then began coughing loudly. As Reverend Davenport slapped her firmly on the back, there was a ripple of polite applause from the rest of the audience. Jo slunk back to her seat.

GOING TO THE pub after the meeting had been Lucy's idea. She'd flapped away Meera's comment that she didn't really drink.

"Come on, just for one—let's make the most of having babysitters, although Freddie hates me calling them that."

"Who's babysitting?" asked Rachel.

"Joan and Bill. They are at Meera's house and I brought Freddie round to meet Krish too," explained Lucy.

"I don't usually leave Krish with people I don't know, but they seemed like very nice people and Joan told me about her background as a district nurse, so she understood all my notes about Krish's inhalers," explained Meera.

"And it will be good for Krish to know someone in his class before he starts school," reasoned Rachel.

"Oh, I think they're going to get along fabulously," declared Lucy. "Freddie blurted out the story of the puppies being born on my bed and Krish wanted to know every gory detail." She laughed and turned to Jo, who had been lighting a cigarette and trying to zone out this dull discussion about childcare. "You'll come won't you, Jo?" she asked.

"Sure, why not," replied Jo, blowing out a plume of smoke. Unlike Meera she could kill for a drink after that parish council meeting.

LUCY WENT STRAIGHT to the bar while Rachel introduced Jo and Meera to some of the regulars, half of whom she seemed to be related to, before the three of them found a table in the window. Jo had never seen the point of small talk, but Meera appeared keen to start a conversation.

"Jo, did you know Rachel and I were at university together? I was quite surprised to find her here. She'd always planned to work abroad. Isn't that right, Rachel?" she began.

"Yes, but life doesn't always work out the way you planned," said Rachel, fiddling with the edge of a beer mat.

"You can say that again," muttered Jo in agreement. The three of them sat in silence for a few minutes, before Meera tried again.

"So," she said, "last night I began reading *Pride and Prejudice* for what must be the ninth or tenth time. Are either of you Austen fans?"

"Not really, Meera," replied Rachel, shaking her head and looking apologetic. "I had to read it for A-level English, but I couldn't help thinking the five sisters could be doing so much more with their lives than simply sitting around waiting for a man to marry them, especially Lizzy."

"Oh, I always considered it a more romantic time, in those days," said Meera, sounding a little crestfallen. "Do you agree, Jo?"

"No," said Jo with a grimace. "I was made to read all the classics too—Austen, the Brontës, Dickens—but I couldn't see the romance either. All I ever thought was everyone would be a lot happier if they had decent plumbing and penicillin."

"Don't listen to them, Meera," said Lucy, who had arrived at the table carrying a tray with four glasses and a bottle of prosecco, even though Meera had requested a mineral water and Jo a beer. "I loved *Pride and Prejudice* and always dreamt Darcy would sweep me off my feet one day."

"Really? Me too. When did you last read it?" asked Meera.

Rachel raised an eyebrow at Lucy, who flushed in embarrassment as she began to pour the wine.

"Well, to be quite honest, I'm not much of a reader," she admitted, leading to a snort from Rachel. "I was thinking more of the TV version, you know the one with Colin Firth in his dripping wet shirt. I can't remember much else."

Meera smiled politely and gave a small cough before attempting to start another conversation. Jo had to hand it to her, she was certainly tenacious.

"Colonel Marsden asked me if I wanted to join the parish council," Meera said. "I didn't want to appear rude, but I really don't think I have enough spare time. Do you think I should have said yes? I mean, it was a nice welcoming gesture."

"Don't worry about it, Meera," said Rachel. "There's a spare seat on the council. They've been trying to co-opt someone for ages. I suggest you say no, unless you want to die of boredom. They once took three hours to decide what colour to paint the door of the village hall."

"Christ, I hope they don't ask me to join," said Jo with a shudder. The other three burst out laughing.

"I don't think there's any danger of that," said Rachel. "They'll probably all be having nightmares after your talk."

"Was I too blunt?" asked Jo in surprise. She was genuinely unaware that her talk wasn't what the parish councillors might have been expecting.

"Put it this way, I doubt you will be asked to come and chat with the children at school," said Rachel to more sniggering from Lucy and Meera.

Jo smiled good-naturedly. "Okay, okay, I guess I'm more used to being in the interview room than doing public relations," she admitted.

"The best bit was when you said 'crackhead' and the racist lady nearly choked on her custard cream." Meera laughed, then clapped her hand to her mouth.

"I quite envied the rev," said Lucy wiping the tears from her eyes. "I've been wanting to thump Nora Parkin for years." She raised her glass. "How about a toast? To new friends and new beginnings."

"New beginnings," echoed the others. They all took a drink and Jo tried hard not to pull a face as the fizzy, sweet liquid washed over her tongue. She was definitely not a prosecco girl.

"So, what brings you to Hartwell, Jo?" asked Rachel.

"My own stupidity," replied Jo grimly, then looking at the three expectant faces realised they wanted more. She sighed. "I mucked up a big arrest and the suspect had to be released. It was either get demoted or come here."

"What about your family? They must miss you?" asked Rachel and Jo noticed her exchange a quick look with Lucy.

"I don't have a family," she replied bluntly, wondering if there was any way she could avoid where this conversation was bound to lead. She always found it was better to be open about her past, but she hated the inevitable awkwardness that followed. However, this lot seemed to be the types who would keep banging on about her family if she didn't tell; far better to get it over and done with. Like ripping off a plaster. She took a deep breath. "I was abandoned outside Great Ormond Street Hospital when I was a few hours old. They never traced my mother."

Her statement was met with silence. Then suddenly Lucy flung her arms around her.

"Oh, you poor, poor thing! You're a foundling!" she gasped, hugging her tightly.

"I'm so sorry, Jo," said Meera, her eyes glistening with tears as she took Jo's hand. Jo held herself rigid until they both let her go. She was used to dealing with teasing and banter, but not this outpouring of feminine sympathy. Usually, she was the only female in a team full of testosterone-driven males, who at the most would give her an awkward slap on the back.

"Hence your surname?" asked Rachel, after a brief pause.

"Got it in one," replied Jo. "The nurse who named me didn't have the greatest imagination." She downed the rest of her drink and stood up to leave. There had been quite enough bonding with the locals for one night. Besides she couldn't drink any more of that girly, fizzy crap. There were a couple of beers chilling in the fridge back at the cottage. "Cheers for the drink. I'll see you all around."

Ignoring the chorus of "Oh, are you sure?" and "Well goodnight then!" that followed her, she put her head down and stepped out into the eerily quiet village and retreated to her new home.

CHAPTER FIVE

THE NEXT MORNING Lucy was in a panic yet again. Crawling along on her hands and knees she was hunting around the floor of the village hall, searching for her mobile phone. She had only realised it was missing when she was getting ready for bed the night before, feeling relieved as she brushed her teeth that despite Jo's unsettling self-defence talk, it was clear she wasn't in Hartwell to grill her, or anyone else, about Rupert. She'd then gone to plug her phone in to charge, only to find it wasn't in her bag. She had turned Hartwell Hall upside down looking for it.

First thing that morning, she'd phoned Jack to ask if she'd left it in the pub, but he said there was no sign of it. In desperation, she'd retraced her steps and ended up at the village hall. She could definitely remember turning it on to vibrate as she walked down to the meeting with Meera and Jo. She peered under the row of chairs, no luck there. Standing up she went to where the committee had been sitting on the stage. If only she could whistle for it like she did when one of the dogs disappeared. Moving the long curtains to one side, she suddenly spotted it lying on the floor. Breathing a huge sigh of relief, she picked it up. The battery had almost run out, but it was still working. How on earth did it get there though? She must have dropped it when she was rifling through her bag, looking for Freddie's timetable. Carefully she slipped it into her pocket, stepped outside, and locked the door of the village hall securely behind her. She'd practically had to beg Nora for the keys. She would never hear the end of it if the place wasn't left exactly as she'd found it.

As she walked away from the village hall, she glanced across to what had once been an old hay barn. Over the last year, she had watched from a distance, as it was gradually converted into a house. Today, however, the white vans belonging to the teams of builders and workmen were nowhere to be seen. Surely it wouldn't do any harm to take a quick look. Feeling nervous, she inched past the empty pickup truck parked on the verge and pushed open the freshly painted five-bar gate bearing the new slate sign engraved with the name: "The Hayloft". The original mellow cream stone walls had been preserved, but one side of the building was now entirely made of glass. It meant the place would be filled with natural light and whoever lived there would have breath-taking views over the moors. Lucy cupped her hands on either side of her face and pressed her nose up against the glass to try and see inside.

"You do know you're trespassing, don't you?"

Lucy spun around in horror. A tall, dark-haired man was leaning against the pickup truck, his arms folded. It was the same man she had seen Ben and Dan with at the quiz. That's why he was familiar. He was Rob Harrison, the local boy turned successful property developer. After making a fortune in Leeds, converting old industrial buildings into luxury apartments, he had returned to Hartwell, his childhood home. Since then, he'd been busy buying up land and derelict farm buildings. Apparently, he'd left the village when he was a teenager and Lucy had heard a rumour that he'd been in prison.

"I'm so terribly sorry," she stammered, her face turning bright red as she backed away from the window.

"I was joking," he said with a slight twitch of his lips. He unfolded his arms and crunched across the gravel driveway towards her. "If you want to see inside properly, I could give you a guided tour."

"Oh, um that would be lovely, if it's not too much trouble, thank you. As you've probably guessed I'm quite nosy," she gabbled, as she always did when she was embarrassed or nervous. Rob didn't reply as she followed him round to the side of the house and through the heavy oak front door.

"Wow this is amazing," gasped Lucy as she stepped into the double-height hallway. The building itself might be a couple of hundred years old, but there were no creaking floorboards or walls discoloured by patches of damp here. Everywhere she looked was pale wood, glass, and chrome. Downstairs was open plan with the sitting and dining areas focused on the incredible view. A floating staircase led up to galleried landing on the first floor. Lucy wandered around open-mouthed then became aware that Rob was watching her intently with his inky blue eyes.

"I thought it would be a bit modern for your tastes," he said, "what with you living in a stately home and everything."

Lucy looked at him in surprise. "No, no not at all. After

all you can like Mozart as much as Madonna, can't you?"

Rob shrugged. "I can't say I'm a fan of either."

Lucy nodded. She could have guessed that. With his jet-black hair that fell forward across his face, and in his jeans and black T-shirt, he looked like he was probably into guitar-led, heavy rock music. Below his sleeve, she could just make out the edge of a tattoo peeping out on what she had to admit was a very well-toned bicep. The only hint at his financial success was the expensive watch on his wrist.

"You okay?" he asked.

Oh God she'd been staring. She blushed again. "Oh absolutely, just you know, err, admiring everything. The fabulous view and look in here," she said hurrying through into the kitchen area. "I'd adore one of these granite islands and you even have one of those taps that give you instant boiling water," she twittered on, while all the time thinking, *Shut up, Lucy. You sound like Max trying to flog the place.* Rob had followed her and was now leaning against the huge, chrome drinks fridge.

"I heard you were looking to have some work done up at the hall; maybe you could get one installed yourself."

"If only," sighed Lucy. "I need to stop the water running down the walls first."

"It's that bad?"

"Afraid so," replied Lucy, raking her fingers through her hair.

"Any particular reason you only got quotes from Leeds firms and none of the local builders? I would have thought they'd be cheaper."

Lucy shrugged. "I don't know really. Max has been sorting it all for me."

Rob raised an eyebrow. "Does Max know much about building?"

"I assume so. Rupert let him take care of everything like that."

"I see," replied Rob, looking like he wanted to say more on the subject, but instead he said, "I hear you have new tenants. You must be pleased. Maintaining empty properties can be a massive drain on an estate like yours."

Lucy nodded, pleased for the change in subject. She felt awkward talking about Rupert here.

"Yes, it's such a relief. One less problem, and a doctor and a police officer—it doesn't get much better than that."

"Because they are professionals you mean? I suppose that's important to you," said Rob, with a slight edge to his voice.

"Yes," confirmed Lucy hesitantly. Why had he made their professions sound like a dirty word? Maybe if he really had been to prison, he didn't like the police. Actually, if he had been to prison should she be alone here with him? They stood in silence for a moment. Silences always made her feel uncomfortable, but it didn't seem to bother him. "I should probably be going," she said finally.

"You don't want to see upstairs?"

"Maybe another time."

He gave a shrug and she followed him back outside.

"So, are you all finished now?" she asked as he locked the door behind them.

"I thought I was, but the building inspector wants us to put the overhead electric cables that feed the garage, underground." He pointed to a new stone-built structure in the corner of the plot nearest the village hall. "While we're digging again, I thought I might make an opening in the boundary wall for a gate. If we built a footbridge over the stream, it would give direct access to the moors. Do you want to see what I mean?"

Lucy felt a shiver run through her. She took a step back and shook her head. "No, thanks. I really should go and give these keys back to Nora. Thanks for the tour though."

"No problem. See you around," he called after her, frowning slightly as Lucy turned and hurried away.

WHEN SHE ARRIVED at the village shop, Lucy gave Nora the friendliest smile she could muster.

"Thank you very much for lending me the keys," she said politely, handing them over. Nora took them and made an exaggerated show of checking each one, as if she expected Lucy to have damaged them in the half hour they'd been in her possession.

"You're making quite a habit of losing things. Find your phone, did you?" she asked.

"Yes, Mrs Parkin, I did luckily," replied Lucy through gritted teeth.

"Well, that's something I suppose."

Just then the doorbell jangled, and Guy strode in.

"Good day, ladies. May I have my copy of the *Racing Post* please, Mrs P?"

Nora ducked down behind the counter and Lucy gratefully took his arrival as an excuse to leave. However, no sooner had she escaped the village shop, than she turned down the lane by the church to see her mother-in-law heading towards her.

"Have you found homes for those puppies yet?" asked Caroline, waving away Lucy's attempt to kiss her hello. She had been horrified when she'd discovered Tilly had been allowed to give birth not just in the master bedroom, but on the four-poster bed which, she had informed Lucy three times, dated from the reign of Queen Anne.

"Well, I promised Freddie we would keep one. You know how much he adores dogs."

As always Caroline thawed a little at the mention of her grandson. "Yes, it seems unlike most of the Hanleys, he has a kind heart. What about the others?"

"There's only one left. Two are going to be staying in the village. I didn't like the idea of handing Tilly's babies over to strangers. They feel like family."

Caroline's expression turned arctic again. "Really, Lucinda! You are far too sentimental."

Before Lucy could respond, Caroline turned on her heel and stalked across the road to the dower house. Lucy flopped down on to the low stone wall and closed her eyes with a groan. What a day!

"Are you in the bad books again?" asked a friendly voice beside her. Lucy looked up and saw Guy smiling down at her.

"Am I ever anywhere else?" She sighed.

"Only with your mother-in-law. Now, how about we cheer you up with a drink at the Hart, before it's time for you to pick up Freddie," he asked offering her his hand.

"That would be lovely. Between losing my phone, Caroline and Nora, it's been quite a day," she said letting him pull her to her feet. They linked arms and together they strolled over to the pub.

Lucy took a seat at one of the small tables on the cobbles outside while Guy went inside to get the drinks. She said hello to Jack and Ben, who were enjoying a pint at the next table.

"Did you find out if Jo's single when you were talking last night?" asked Jack.

Lucy grinned at him, but shook her head. "Sorry, no. I don't think girly chats are quite her thing."

"You're wasting your time, Jack," said Ben. "A woman like her will chew you up and spit you out."

"What a way to go though." Jack sighed.

"I thought the doctor seemed very nice," said Ben, turning to Lucy. She gave him a sympathetic smile.

"Well as far as I know Meera is married," she said.

Ben blushed furiously. "Oh, I didn't mean anything by it," he said, quickly, "just you know, that's she's nice." He adjusted glasses. "In the village hall, she sounded very professional."

Shirley snorted as she followed Guy outside with a tray of drinks. "Professional! What are they like, Lucy?" she said with a grin. "A couple of attractive women arrive in the village and they turned into schoolboys, again."

"Now don't be too harsh on them, Shirley." Guy laughed. "Even an old fossil like me can remember what it's like to be young and in love."

"Don't be silly," said Lucy, kindly, "you're not an old fossil."

Guy beamed at her. "Well in that case, my dear, a toast. To love."

LATER THAT EVENING, Lucy was busy putting the various buckets, saucepans, and bowls in position. The day had been warm and muggy, but the threat of a thunderstorm hung heavily in the air. Suddenly Freddie shouted down to her.

"Mum! Mum! I think there's a man out in the yard."

"It's all right, darling. It's probably Bill," she called back whilst silently cursing Jared Parkin. Nora's grandson had taken great delight in scaring all the other children in the playground that lunchtime with tales of the Druids, who once lived in the village, coming back as zombies. Freddie was a serious little boy and easily influenced. The previous week, she'd let him watch a film about an alien invasion and he'd spent the rest of the evening peering out of his bedroom window, convinced there was a strange light moving around the garden. The incident today had been made even worse by Jared singling Freddie out and telling him that, as he was a Hanley, the Druid zombies would come for him first.

Lucy jumped as the cellar door loudly creaked open, and Bill appeared at the top of the steps.

"Sorry, did I startle you, Lady H? I was down there trying to fix a fuse. The lights in the west wing have all blown," he explained.

"Oh dear! Not again. Any luck?" asked Lucy, shuffling

the last bucket into position with her foot.

"I'm afraid not," said Bill closing the cellar door behind him. "We might need an electrician to take a look, this time. I think it's the wiring that's gone."

Lucy sighed. More bad news. She was going to have to come up with a way to generate some income and soon.

"By the way, Bill, have you just been out in the yard?" she asked.

Bill shook his head. "No, Lady H." He nodded towards the cellar door. "I've been down there over half an hour. Why?"

"Freddie thought he saw someone," Lucy replied. "It's probably just his imagination, but…"

Bill patted her on the arm. "Let's go and take a look to be sure, before I go."

The two of them went into the kitchen. Bill opened the back door. Outside it was still almost light enough to see, but he took the torch from his toolbox and swung it from corner to corner and down towards the drive.

"No sign of anyone, Lady H, and all the gates are shut. I shouldn't worry too much. I'm sure the dogs would soon let you know if you had a prowler."

"Yes, you're probably right," Lucy agreed, giving him a hug goodbye, although actually she wasn't so sure. Tilly had always been the guard dog of the house, but right now she was too preoccupied with her puppies. As for Pickle, he was next to useless. He was currently upstairs with Freddie, eating the shortbread Joan had sent with Bill. She locked and bolted the back door behind Bill, then went to check the front door, the side door, and the garden door.

On her way back down the corridor to the reception hall she passed the umbrella stand that had been filled with all sorts of paraphernalia over the years. Recalling Jo's words of advice, she fished out her old hockey stick. She might not have played since her school days, but she was still capable of giving someone a decent thwack to protect herself and her son. Then she trudged upstairs to her office and added 'call an electrician' to her ever-growing to-do list.

Chapter Six

"MUM, MUM, COME quick!" Meera's eyes shot open at the sound of her son's voice. It was a little after eight in the morning and she'd been enjoying slumbering in bed, still exhausted after all the unpacking, but now she leapt up and dashed downstairs.

"What's wrong?" she asked breathlessly, when she found Krish in the kitchen. The back door was open, and he was wearing his winter gloves and had something clasped in his hands.

"I found it out in the garden. I think it flew into the window and hurt itself." Carefully he opened his hands a little to reveal a tiny bat. Meera recoiled in horror.

"Oh, Krish, I don't think you should be touching that. It might have rabies or something."

"Don't be silly, Mum. There's hardly any rabies in this country—you know that. Besides I put my gloves on to be safe. I think it's just a baby and it's wing looks like it might be broken. Can you fix it?"

"I can only really fix humans, Krish," she replied looking around for her phone. Never having had any pets, she was always a little nervous around animals, but being out in the countryside, maybe there was some sort of rescue service she could call. Then through the window she spotted two men chatting outside the farmhouse across the road. She recognised the tall one wearing glasses as the local vet. Rachel had introduced her to him at the pub the other night. What was his name again? Ben something? Bannister, that was it. She rushed out of the front door and on to the cobbles.

"Good morning," she called, waving her arm above her head, "Hello! Mr Bannister, can you help me please?"

The two men turned around and Meera was suddenly acutely aware she was in her fluffy pink dressing gown and slippers, but before she could duck back inside, Ben came striding over towards her.

"Hello, Dr. Kumar. What's the problem?" he asked in his soft Scottish accent. He was almost a foot taller than her, with short light brown hair that stood up at odd angles and he wore glasses that were held together with Sellotape in one corner.

"My son, Krish, has found an injured bat and I'm not sure what to do," she began to explain.

"She can only fix humans," said a small voice behind her. Krish had followed her to the door, still cradling the bat. Before she had a chance to introduce him, Ben was kneeling down peering at the injured animal.

"Hello, Krish. I'm Ben and I'm a vet. What have you got there?" he asked with a friendly smile.

"I think it's a pipistrelle with a broken wing," said Krish, slowly opening his hand a little more.

"I think you're right," agreed Ben. "Do you know much about bats, Krish?"

"I know there are eighteen species in this country and the

pipistrelle is the most common."

Meera stood watching them talk, relieved that the vet was taking her son seriously. She was worried he might have told Krish he should have left it where he found it and let nature take its course.

"That's right and well done for putting on gloves before you picked him up. Are you okay holding on to him a bit longer, while I go and grab my bag from the car?" said Ben standing up and adjusting his glasses.

"Are going to put it out of its misery?" asked Meera in a hushed voice.

"Mum!" exclaimed Krish.

"I'm only asking."

Ben smiled and shook his head. "No, but I am going to give the poor wee chap something for the pain."

Meera ushered Krish back inside the house, while Ben went to his car, returning a few seconds later. He entered the kitchen and immediately banged his head on one of the low wooden beams.

"Oh dear, are you all right?" asked Meera.

"Fine," he replied, straightening his glasses. "I do it all the time. Most of the places around here were built when people were much shorter."

Meera and Krish both watched silently as Ben carefully took the tiny bat from Krish and administered the injection. Despite his size and slightly chaotic appearance, he was surprisingly gentle.

"Have you got something we could put him in? A shoe-box perhaps? Then we'll need to put something soft inside like a tea towel and a bottle lid with some water in it so he can have a drink."

"I'll go and find a shoebox," said Krish immediately dashing upstairs. Ben turned to Meera and grinned.

"That's quite the animal lover you have there. Is it only bats he's interested in?"

Meera shook her head as she opened the drawer where her tea towels were neatly folded.

"No, anything with a pulse, from mice to elephants. He loves living out here. He spends every second staring out of the window instead of at the TV screen and I'm provided with a running commentary of the lives of our new neighbours, the sheep, and the rooks."

Ben laughed. "I was just the same at his age."

At that moment, Krish returned slightly breathless with one of Meera's designer shoeboxes. No doubt her favourite and most expensive kitten heels had been dumped out on to the floor, but she didn't say anything as she handed him a tea towel and the top from a bottle of water. She was happy to see him so engrossed in helping the little creature.

"Will you need to operate?" he asked, as Ben carefully laid the bat in the box.

"I'm not sure, but there's a wildlife rescue centre in Helmsley and the lady who runs it is a bit of a bat expert. I'd like her to take a look at him."

"Can I come too?" asked Krish eagerly.

"You can if your mum doesn't mind? I could drive us all there and you could hold the box for me."

Two pairs of expectant eyes turned to Meera. So much for enjoying a leisurely morning.

"Okay, okay give me two minutes to get dressed," she

said. A little over an hour later, the three of them were sitting in Helmsley marketplace eating ice creams. They had left the baby bat at the wildlife centre, with the lady there promising to keep him under observation and report back to Ben if the wing didn't improve. Then Ben had given them a tour of the other animals there: dehydrated hedgehogs, a three-legged toad, an injured fox cub, even an elderly one-eyed badger. Meera didn't think she'd ever seen Krish so excited.

"So, Krish," asked Ben, a trickle of mint choc chip running down his chin, "do you want to work with animals when you're older?"

"Yes, I want to be a vet like you," replied Krish immediately.

"Good man." Ben laughed.

"Not a doctor like me?" asked Meera innocently.

"No," replied Krish, "it's like you said, you can only fix humans. Ben can fix all sorts of animals."

"He's got a point," said Ben grinning across at Meera.

"Two against one isn't fair," she replied as she delicately spooned another mouthful of vanilla out of her tub.

After they'd finished their ice cream. Ben showed Krish how to play Poohsticks on the bridge over the River Rye. With her sunglasses on, Meera could watch the two of them without looking like she was staring. Krish jumped in the air with joy as his stick appeared first and Meera suddenly felt a pang of sadness. He should have been doing this with his father. How on earth could Dev be so selfish?

"WOW IT'S AS big as a castle!" exclaimed Krish, as they approached Hartwell Hall. It was about a week after the bat incident and Lucy had invited Krish over to play with Freddie while Meera had a handover meeting with Dr. Robertson. Meera had purposely left the previous week free to concentrate on turning the cottage into a home, while Krish settled in at school. She had been far more nervous about her son arriving mid-term than he was, but she need not have worried. Krish had been thrilled to find himself in the same class as Freddie. The two boys were becoming firm friends and Rachel had assured her that he had covered everything that her class had studied on the curriculum so far that year.

As her little Fiat 500 crunched down the long gravel driveway, Meera had to agree with her son, Hartwell Hall was huge. It was also very beautiful, just like the houses in some of her favourite books. When she was a little girl growing up in India, she had devoured all the English classic novels. A little after her tenth birthday, her father had announced the family was moving to England, so he could help an uncle run his garment factory, and Meera had eagerly imagined strolling through meadows and along cobbled streets, wearing long dresses and taking tea in elegant houses. The tiny two-bedroomed terrace backing on to the M62 on the outskirts of Bradford had come as quite a disappointment.

A year or so later, they had moved to a slightly bigger house and Meera no longer had to share a bedroom with Nishit, her younger brother. Her father worked long hours, her mother tried to adjust to their new life in this grey, damp country, and Meera threw herself into her schoolwork. Any holidays were spent driving up and down motorways to visit relatives, who lived in the suburbs of Birmingham or Sheffield or occasionally returning to India to see her grandparents.

As the years past, she'd almost given up ever finding her dream of England. Then she'd met Rachel at university. Looking at the photos of her new friend's home village, she realised such places really did exist. A few months ago, exhausted after working up to eighteen hours a day, jabbing arms and convincing reluctant patients that the vaccine was safe, she'd seen the advert for the vacancy in Hartwell and knew it was fate.

Now as they pulled up at the impressive front entrance of Hartwell Hall, the romantic in her could almost believe Mr Rochester would stride out to greet her. However, Lucy, Freddie, and a small yapping dog came tumbling out instead. Meera was quite anxious about Krish being so close to all the dogs Lucy owned, but Lucy had assured her that the boys would spend most of their time outside in the fresh air. Meera knew Krish wouldn't be able to stay away from the puppies though, so she'd sent him armed with both inhalers and checked that Joan would be on hand in case of an emergency. Still as she drove away down the long gravel drive, she couldn't help but worry. Her little boy was her whole world.

MEERA'S JAW WAS beginning to ache from smiling for so

long. This meeting with Dr. Robertson was meant to be a straightforward handover before he retired. So far, she had been there two hours and all she'd heard about was his gout and golf handicap. Finally, he left with a cheery wave and Meera could begin her work.

Part one of her mission to drag the surgery into the twenty-first century was to make sure all the medical records were uploaded on to the computer. It was shocking how antiquated the system was. Neither of the medical secretaries at the surgery seemed very keen of her ideas to modernise the place. They were far more interested in Meera's personal life and the whereabouts of Krish's father. Meera told them what she told anybody who asked. Her husband was away on business in India. It was all she was prepared to say and all they needed to know.

Not wanting to think about Dev right now, she turned her attention back to the medical records. She yanked open another drawer of the ancient filing cabinet, only to send the pile of files perched on top falling to the floor and scattering their contents across the room. With a groan of exasperation, she dropped to her knees and began collecting up all the loose papers. As she did so, she noticed it was the H pile that had fallen, and she was picking up Lucinda's medical notes. Automatically, her eyes began to scan down. She'd had an alarming collection of injuries over the last few years. Cracked ribs, a badly bruised eye that needed to be treated, a sprained wrist, a scalded arm. Next to most entries, in Dr. Robertson's barely legible scrawl, were the words: 'due to horse riding accident'.

Meera leaned back against the filing cabinet, feeling

slightly sick. Lucy had never mentioned owning a horse, and in Meera's experience, her injures were more likely due to someone with two legs not four. If she had seen these injuries at her previous inner-city practice, her first assumption would have been that the woman was a victim of domestic violence. Sadly, far too many of her patients had suffered at the hands of their husbands or boyfriends.

She was stunned. Could lovely, bubbly, outgoing Lucy have been suffering like all those other poor women? Quickly, she checked the dates. The last injury, the scalding, had been only a day before the first lockdown and before her husband had disappeared. The two secretaries had lost no time, filling her in on this piece of local gossip, when they heard who was looking after Krish.

Meera continued to read. Lucy hadn't need to visit the doctor since the scalding. A hundred thoughts began swimming through her head, then a particularly horrible one floated to the top. She leaned forwards and rummaged through the papers still scattered on the floor, until she found the notes for Freddie. Holding her breath, she began reading through. There were the usual records for childhood immunisations, a bout of chicken pox and a nasty throat infection that required antibiotics. Nothing untoward, except for the last entry. He had needed treatment for a scald on his arm too, at the same time as his mother. She checked to see if Dr. Robertson had asked for an explanation, as she would have done. She squinted and could just about make out 'accident helping mother cook pasta'. Meera felt sick. She could hear Lucy's voice, in her head, imagining what she would have said to Robertson.

"Stupid, clumsy me. I'm so terribly sorry, Freddie darling. I should never have said he could help, Doctor."

But what if it wasn't Lucy who should be apologising?

BY FIVE O'CLOCK Meera was exhausted. With some relief, she locked her office door behind her, but she couldn't shut out what she'd read about Lucy. She still hadn't decided if she should say or do anything. To make matters more complicated, she had invited her new friends round for supper. They would be arriving in less than two hours.

As she walked home, she thought about the others. It wasn't only Lucy she was worried about, Rachel seemed like a shadow of her former self. The two of them had met for coffee earlier in the week. Meera had been looking forward to chatting about their time at university, but Rachel didn't appear in the mood to reminisce and although she'd cracked the odd joke, she seemed to have lost all the enthusiasm and energy she'd had as a student.

Then there was Jo. Like Meera, her new neighbour had a week or so before she started her new job. Meera had been busy finishing her unpacking and doing little DIY jobs and had called in a couple of times to see how Jo was settling in. Jo, however, didn't seem very interested in making her cottage into a home. The walls and shelves remained bare, with no sign of any personal effects. Meera had been particularly shocked by the kitchen. From what she could see, it looked like Jo existed on a diet of crisps and coffee. When she asked if Jo didn't enjoy cooking, she'd simply shrugged and admitted she preferred takeaways. Meera, who loved to cook, had immediately invited her round for a murgh makhani, one of her specialities. For once Krish hadn't complained about her cooking Indian food. He'd been thrilled to meet a real-life police officer, especially one from London, but their first encounter had sounded more like an interrogation.

"Have you ever arrested anyone?" he'd asked eagerly.

"Yes," Jo had replied without further elaboration.

"Ever been in a police car with the siren going?"

"Yes."

"Do you wear a stab vest?"

"Sometimes."

"Ever been stabbed?"

"No."

This had continued for nearly twenty minutes, before Meera stepped in and told Krish to leave their guest in peace.

"Sorry," Jo had apologised with a shrug as a disappointed Krish disappeared upstairs, "I'm not great with children."

Meera sighed now as she turned the key in her front door. Without her family nearby, Meera had hoped to form a little support network with these other single women in the village, but they weren't making it easy.

Once she was inside the cottage, she changed out of her dark suit into a linen dress and began to prepare supper. Cooking always helped her to relax and she had decided to make chicken balti with rice and naan bread, and some samosas to start with. It was a lovely summer's evening, and she propped the back door open. She had already moved the kitchen table and chairs out into the garden and now she lit some citronella candles to ward off the midges that tended to congregate close to the climbing roses at dusk.

Ben had helped her hang some fairy lights on the old apple tree. He'd called around the day before to update Krish on the bat. Apparently, there was no need for surgery and the little creature was healing well. The two of them had spent half an hour trying to locate where the bats might be roosting, while Meera wobbled and swayed on top of a stepladder until Ben offered to assist. He'd dismissed her thanks with a wave of his hand.

"It's fine. Besides, you're too short to be able to do it properly," he'd said matter-of-factly. Meera had been a little taken aback at his bluntness at first, but soon realised it was just his way. Dev would never have told her she was too short. He would have said something smooth like: "You are too delicate to be exerting yourself."

At first, she'd found this charming; now she would take direct over smooth any day. Ben had also helped her move the tables and chairs outside, then he'd stayed for supper. They'd chatted about the pressure of having a job that meant you were often on call and then he'd helped Krish make paper aeroplanes, coming up with designs inspired by the shape of different birds' wings.

"THESE CANDLES ARE great, Meera," said Jo helping herself to another samosa. "I usually need to light a ciggie to keep the midges away or they eat me alive."

"Then I guess you must be blood type O," said Meera,

placing some naan bread on the table.

"Yeh, O negative," replied Jo.

"Hey so's my mum. She's always donating blood or at least she was pre-Covid. And come to think of it, the midges always go for her too," said Rachel, who had arrived at the same time as Jo.

"Midges and mosquitoes love people who are type O. They also like alcohol," continued Meera with a slight smile as Jo took another sip of her beer.

"Well, I'm not giving up the booze. I'd rather be bitten," replied Jo, shuffling her chair closer to the candle.

Lucy, with Freddie and Krish in tow, was the last to arrive bearing flowers and wine. Freddie and Krish immediately disappeared upstairs.

"Supper will be ready in ten minutes," Meera called after them.

"I doubt they're hungry," said Lucy, kissing Meera on the cheek. "They've been eating Joan's scones all afternoon." Meera frowned slightly, and Lucy quickly added, "But they did have masses of fruit salad after lunch too."

Lucy paused and looked around the cottage sitting room. Chunky white candles were artistically arranged in the fireplace, delicate pencil sketches lined the walls and Meera had draped brightly coloured scarves over the plain white sofas.

"Wow, you've really transformed the place, Meera. It looks amazing! So fresh and modern. If the career in medicine hadn't worked out, you would have made a fabulous interior decorator."

"Thank you," replied Meera. She had always loved art

and design, but her parents would never have let her study something so frivolous. She could clearly remember the parents' evening when she was due to choose her GCSE options. She'd sat opposite the careers teacher with her mother and father on either side. It was unusual for them both to attend such events, but as it became clear to them that Nish was unlikely to fulfil the academic ambitions they had for their children, they had to pin all their hopes on their daughter.

"So, Meera," Miss Calver had begun, kindly, "you are achieving Grade As in all subjects, so the world really is your oyster. Where do you see yourself in the future?"

Before Meera could reply, her father had leaned across and tapped the desk with his finger, as he often did when he wanted to make an important point.

"She needs to be a doctor or a lawyer."

Miss Calver looked down and began shuffling her papers, obviously embarrassed.

"Right, well, I see. Both noble occupations, but for medicine you would need to continue with all three sciences: Biology, Chemistry, and Physics. What do you think, Meera?"

Meera felt three sets of eyes on her. She had a sudden vision of herself as a sort of Florence Nightingale or Mary Seacole figure, gliding between hospital beds as handsome soldiers blew her kisses, so she dropped History and French and as with so many of her other romantic expectations, she'd been disappointed.

After putting the wine in the fridge and flowers in water, Meera led Lucy out into the garden.

"Sorry, I'm a bit late," said Lucy, kissing the other two on their cheeks. "I had a meeting with a woman from the tourist board about opening the house and she was a bit of a chatterbox."

"Are you thinking of opening the house to the public?" asked Meera handing her a glass of wine.

"Well, I was," said Lucy sitting down next to Rachel. "I opened the gardens for a few months last year and it seemed like a natural progression. But according to the lady with the clipboard, it will cost so much to get it to meet health and safety standards, I'm not sure it'll be worth it. Then there's the staffing costs to think of." She sighed. "So, it looks like I'm going to have to come up with something else. Any ideas, ladies?"

"What did you do before you were married?" asked Meera. "Maybe you could return to that in some way."

Lucy wrinkled her forehead. "Gosh, I don't think I did much except have a good time. I barely scraped through my GCSEs, then Daddy sent me to secretarial college, but I never learnt to type with more than two fingers. The last actual job I had was as the receptionist at an art gallery on Cork Street. I didn't do much except smile at customers and organise the drinks and canapés if they were holding an exhibition. I think I spent most of the time painting my nails and chatting to friends who popped by. Then along came Rupert and swept me off my feet."

"Couldn't Daddy help out now?" asked Jo, a note of sarcasm in her voice.

"No." Lucy shook her head sadly. "He died a few years ago, and it turned out he was up to his ears in debt. Rupert was furious. He was rather hoping we'd cash in."

Rachel and Jo both gave an indignant snort and Meera patted her shoulder sympathetically.

"Speaking of Cork Street," said Jo, thoughtfully, "I once went to this house in Mayfair that was being used to shoot a coffee commercial and they were being paid a fortune. You could see if a film or TV company want to use your place as a location. The house I went to were charging twenty grand a day."

"Wow!" exclaimed Lucy, her eyes lighting up.

"Unfortunately, one of the actors they hired was an alcoholic," continued Jo. "He got into an argument with the director and either fell or was pushed from the second-floor window—we never found out which. He ended up getting impaled on the railings outside. It took the paramedics over an hour to remove him."

The other three winced in unison, as Jo casually took another drink of her beer.

"How are the puppies doing, Luce?" asked Rachel.

"Fabulously. Tilly is a wonderful mummy and I swear they double in size every day."

"You know I bet you could get at least a grand for each of them," said Jo. "Do you remember how at the beginning of lockdown loads of people decided to get a puppy and the prices went through the roof? Of course, it led to a rise in dognapping gangs too."

Lucy and Rachel exchanged a look. Jo didn't miss it.

"What?" she demanded.

"Well," said Meera, gently. "All your stories do tend to end in either a long prison sentence or someone's death."

Rachel and Lucy grinned, nodding their heads in agreement.

Jo raised her hands in mock surrender. "Okay, okay, it's not my fault I don't do happy ever afters. In my experience, life isn't like all those books you've got filling your shelves, Meera," she said gesturing to the cottage. "I guess it's what comes of spending six years in the Met, but I still think the puppies would sell for good money."

"I know you're right and I could do with the cash," admitted Lucy, "but it wouldn't feel right selling Tilly's babies. Caroline thinks I'm too sentimental, but it would be like selling one of the family. I would just rather know they were all going to good homes. I've promised Freddie he can keep one. Two of them are going to Jack and the colonel, so that only leaves one needing a home."

"What about weddings?" suggested Meera, then noticing the looks of confusion, "Oh sorry, I'm still thinking of how you could use Hartwell Hall to make money. I agree with Jo, I can quite imagine it as the setting for a period drama, but don't you think it would make a beautiful wedding venue too."

"Actually, that's not a bad idea. The place looked beautiful for my wedding," said Lucy. "And I read somewhere that there's a shortage of venues. It could be really lucrative. I remember when I got married, everything was so expensive. I swear putting the word *wedding* in front, doubles the price of everything."

"You wouldn't even need to open the house; you could

simply hire out the grounds to marquee companies," added Meera, warming to her subject. "We had a marquee in Harlow Carr Gardens in Harrogate for our wedding. Or rather two marquees—we couldn't find a venue big enough for all our guests."

"Are the two of you still together?" asked Lucy, twiddling the stem of her wine glass. "It's just that you don't really mention him, nor does Krish."

Meera took a sip of her mineral water. Trotting out her well-practised line of Dev working away in India wasn't going to be enough for the three women surrounding her. Besides, if they were going to be friends then they deserved to know the truth, or at least some of it.

"We've been living separate lives for years, putting a united front on for both our families. Dev spent most of his time at his apartment in Manchester, while Krish and I stayed in Shipley," she began quietly, "but then the pandemic started. Dev knew I would be working long hours, but instead of coming home to help look after Krish, when lockdown was announced, he told me he would be staying in Manchester with the person he was living with there. He chose them over us."

Lucy reached out and squeezed her hand. "I'm really sorry, Meera," she said gently.

"He sounds like a great guy," muttered Jo.

"But Krish must still miss him," reasoned Rachel.

Meera shook her head slowly. "No, it's sad, but he really doesn't seem to. He hardly ever mentions him. You see even before he moved out, Dev didn't spend that much time with us. At first, he'd say he had to work away, but it soon became obvious it wasn't only his work keeping him from coming home. It's always been just me and Krish. Occasionally, Dev would show up. He'd take Krish to the cinema or bring lots of sweets or presents, but it was like he was a fun uncle not a father."

"It was the same with Rupert," said Lucy quietly. Meera looked at her in surprise. This was the second time she'd mentioned her missing husband tonight. Would she also mention her injuries? Her eyes flicked to Lucy's left hand, and the large collection of bangles she always wore on that wrist, the wrist she now knew had been scalded.

"Not the fun uncle part," Lucy continued. "He stopped being fun a long time ago, but even before he disappeared, he spent most of his time down in London. Freddie sometimes asked about him, but hardly ever." She looked at Meera. "You are right—it's sad, not only for Freddie, but Rupert missed out on such a lot." She turned to Rachel. "Do you remember how excited he was about becoming a father, Rach?"

Rachel nodded, but didn't look up from the pattern on the tablecloth she was tracing with her fingers.

"He seemed to love the idea, but not the reality of sleepless nights and dirty nappies. He said he felt trapped," explained Lucy. "Sometimes I thought it was history repeating itself. My mother could never settle down either. She left Daddy and me when I was baby. Partying was more important to her. That and her string of famous boyfriends. I suppose I was a bit of party girl too when I lived in London. Maybe that's who Rupert thought he was marrying, but as soon as Freddie came along, I knew all I wanted to do was try and give him a happy home." Her voice cracked a little and she took a sip of wine.

"Did Rupert have a job in London? What was he doing down there?" asked Jo.

"Cocaine, mainly," replied Lucy, her lips twisting into a wry smile.

"Oh my goodness!" Meera raised her hand to her mouth. "I thought perhaps he'd met someone else too," she said.

"Maybe he did. I really don't know," replied Lucy with a shrug.

"What do you think has happened to him? Do you think he'll come back?" asked Jo.

There was silence. Lucy dropped her eyes and shrugged.

Finally, Rachel looked up. "Anything's possible I suppose," she said.

Later, when everyone had left, Meera went to kiss Krish goodnight. Her normally quiet little boy was full of non-stop chatter about the puppies and his new best friend Freddie. Then when she flopped into bed, she thought about Lucy, Rachel, and Jo. She'd never really had close friends. Her time had always been consumed by work or family, never able to socialise with colleagues because she had to rush home to Krish, but it had felt right to tell them about Dev living with someone else during lockdown. Maybe in time she would tell them more and she hoped that one day Lucy would feel able to confide in her about her injuries. As she closed her eyes, she wondered if Lucy's toast in the pub was correct, and this really was going to be a new beginning for them all.

CHAPTER SEVEN

THE ANGRY RHYTHMIC beat coming from her AirPods filled Jo's head and fresh air filled her lungs, as her feet hit the smooth round cobbles. Despite her move north, she was maintaining her routine of going for a run early each morning. She wasn't Hartwell's only early riser. The church bells were striking six and Frank, yet another member of the Foxton family, was dropping off a pint of milk on her doorstep as she left the cottage. Then two tractors had trundled by, their drivers raising their hands to her in silent greeting.

Her new route took her up to the church at the top of the village, then round the back of the school, past the pub and down to the gates of Hartwell Hall, before heading back to the cottage. It was a world away from pounding the tarmac and concrete of the dirty, noisy streets of East London. Down there it had been a great way to clear her head before another hectic day at work. Somehow, she couldn't see her job here in North Yorkshire being as stressful. If only she could say the same about the private lives of her new friends.

She'd never had a group of close female friends. As a child, she'd rarely spent more than a few months in the same school or children's homes before being moved on, admittedly usually due to her bad behaviour. Then, when she'd joined the police and especially when she'd moved to the drugs squad, she'd got used to being one of the few females on the team. The banter and jokey camaraderie had suited her. Maybe this was why the others all seemed to think she was too direct, but in her opinion they could all do with being a bit more forthright.

Rachel was obviously mad about Lucy, but nobody in the village ever mentioned it. Meera was stuck in a loveless marriage, but had made no mention of divorcing Dev, who sounded like a complete waste of space. As for Lucy, well her husband was even worse, and Jo was convinced that she knew more about his disappearance than she was letting on. Jo shook her head. Relationships were complicated. She was bloody lucky she only had herself to worry about.

In the shade of the oak trees by the old well, Jo paused to catch her breath and take a sip from her water bottle. Suddenly she was aware of the sound of heavy breathing. She turned to see Jack lumbering towards her. His face was flushed, and he was sweating profusely.

"Morning, lovely!" he gasped, raising his hand in greeting as he came to a halt, half doubled over.

Jo smiled despite herself. "You're out early," she said, gently stretching her quads.

"Yep. I heard you'd started jogging, so I thought I'd join you," he panted.

Jo shook her head. He wasn't her type at all, but she couldn't help feeling flattered. She'd never been pursued so romantically or so literally before. Her love life was a long, messy list of one-night stands with arrogant, moody coppers and the occasional smooth-talking lawyer thrown in. They were loners like her and definitely not the type to arrange quiz nights or any other events to boost morale in their community.

"How's the leg?" she asked.

"Holding up," he assured her despite his obvious limp. "How's everything with you?"

"The sooner I get back to London the better."

"Rachel told me you're not exactly happy about being moved up here."

"You can say that again."

"I'm sorry," he said resting his bulk on the edge of the well. "I suppose it must be a bit dull after London. What made you want to join the police in the first place?"

Jo surveyed him for a moment, trying to decide if he was really interested. Then thought what the hell, he sounded genuine enough.

"When I was a teenager, I got caught shoplifting. It was only small stuff: lipsticks, sweets, CDs, things other kids had that I wanted. Anyway, the security guard called the police, and this sergeant turned up. Instead of carting me off to the station, he sat me down in the storeroom and just talked to me. He asked me about my life and my background, then he said he could see I had potential, but if I continued on the same path, I'd end up in prison; I'd become another statistic and the system would have won. He said life had dealt me a rotten hand, but the only person who could change it was me. Then he told the store manager that they didn't have enough to charge me and let me go. That's when I decided to join the police. He'd seen something in me that none of my useless social workers or teachers had. He'd been honest with me, and he'd actually done something that had a positive impact on my life."

She glanced across to see if Jack was going to laugh or make a sarky comment like the guys back at the station would have done, but he just gave her a sad smile.

"Wow, what a nice guy. Did the two of you keep in touch?" he asked.

"Yes, he became my mentor, and when he got married and started a family, he asked me to be the godmother to his children."

"Really?"

"No, I never saw him again. Rachel should also have told you I don't do happy endings," she replied, then feeling a little guilty at Jack's disappointed expression: "What about you? Don't you miss playing rugby?" she asked. She had seen all the photos in the pub of Jack proudly wearing his England shirt. She couldn't imagine how she would handle being told she had to give up the job she loved. It was bad enough being sent away from London.

Jack shrugged. "Yeh, I miss it, but there's nothing I can do about it, so I have to make the best of what I've got. Running my own pub, entertaining people, providing the odd shoulder to cry on, being part of the community—all things considered, it's not so bad. In fact, if I could ever get you to go out with me, my life would be perfect."

Jo barked out a laugh and shook her head. "Don't you ever give up?"

"God loves a trier," he replied with a grin.

"Then you should be the Pope by now." She took a last sip of water. "Come on, I'll race you back."

"I'll let you have a head start," Jack called after her as she sprinted off.

LATER THAT MORNING, Jo sat in front of Chief Constable Carmichael, self-consciously sipping her tea at the North Yorkshire Police Headquarters in Northallerton. She'd abandoned her usual uniform of cargo pants and vest and had changed into a black trouser suit for the meeting. Back in London, when a senior officer called you for a chat, you knew you were in for an almighty bollocking. Jo had certainly been on the receiving end of plenty back at the Met. However, here in North Yorkshire, it seemed that a chat accompanied by tea and biscuits was all that was required. So far, the chief had only told her about his love of cricket and birdwatching. Jo hadn't needed to contribute much more than nods and smiles.

"So how are you finding life in Hartwell? It's a lovely little village. Anything of interest to report?"

"Not much, sir. I've met the parish council and been to the pub once or twice. One of the dogs at Hartwell Hall gave birth to a litter of puppies. That caused quite a stir," she joked to try and illustrate how quiet her new home was, but her boss looked genuinely interested.

"Really? What breed?"

"Erm, it's a black Labrador, I think."

The chief constable nodded thoughtfully. "I promised

my youngest daughter a puppy for her birthday. Let me know if there is still one available, will you?"

"Of course, sir, I'll ask Lucy, that is Lady Hanley. By the way, sir. The disappearance of Lucy's husband, Lord Hanley, is the file still open?"

"Yes indeed, sergeant, as it will be until he is found or until seven years have passed and he is declared dead," he said and stood up. Jo took this to mean she was dismissed. She shook his hand and he wished her well.

"By the way, Sergeant Ormond," he said, when she was almost out the door, "I've picked your first assignment myself. Checking all gun licences of the residents of Hartwell. Technically it's a job for the firearms enquiry officer, but she's off sick and there's quite a backlog. There were no home visits during the pandemic; besides, I thought it would be an excellent way of getting to know the locals."

"Thank you, sir," replied Jo through gritted teeth. Great. Just what she needed! Forget getting to know them, it was more like how to rub the locals up the wrong way. A newcomer knocking on their doors and checking up on their paperwork. Before getting back in her car, her eyes scanned down the names on the surprisingly long list she'd been presented with. There was Guy Lovell, the local MP; Colonel Marsden; two Foxtons who must be yet more of Rachel's relatives; and several names she didn't recognise. It was starting to look like there might actually be more firearms in North Yorkshire than North London, at least legal ones.

At the bottom of the list were the names Lady Caroline Hanley and Lord Rupert Hanley. Jo raised an eyebrow. How would Lucy react to her asking about her missing husband as a police officer not a friend?

A FEW HOURS later and Jo had to hand it to the people up here: they didn't like to waste words. During the first three visits, the farmers she'd met had spoken less than twenty words between them and most of them had been 'Aye' and 'Now then', which she now knew meant hello. Then she'd gone to see Colonel Marsden and Guy Lovell, two southerners, who had more than made up for the farmers' reticence. Both men clearly like the sound of their own voices. The colonel would have given her a blow-by-blow account of every bird he'd ever shot if she'd let him. As for the pompous MP, he had as good as warned her not to visit Hartwell Hall.

"Now, Sergeant, I hope you're not thinking of bothering Lucy with this tiresome business. She's got more than enough to cope with. And it's hardly fair; after all the gun licence is in Rupert's name. Not that I want to tell you your job of course, just a bit of friendly advice."

What a prat! thought Jo as she drove away. Rupert's name was the next one on her list. She may as well get it over with. She gave a low whistle as she drove though the wrought-iron gates. It was the first time she'd seen Hartwell Hall properly. The place was massive. It must cost a fortune to maintain. No wonder Lucy was looking for a way to make it pay. When she rang the front doorbell there was no response, except for the distant sound of a dog barking, so she made the long walk round to the back of the hall. She found Lucy in the courtyard, halfway up a rickety ladder, fiddling with a light above the back door.

"Do you need a hand?" she called out. Lucy turned her

head and smiled.

"Oh hi, Jo! No, I'm okay thanks. I'm replacing this bulb. I promised Freddie I'd do it. He thought he saw someone outside the other night," she explained as she climbed down.

"You had an intruder?" Jo asked with a frown. She'd only been here a few minutes, but she could see Hartwell Hall was a burglar's paradise, with its broken window frames, knackered security lights, and an ancient alarm system.

"No, no, at least I don't think so. He's just got an overactive imagination. You know you actually sounded like the police then," Lucy said with a smile.

Jo shuffled her feet awkwardly. "Actually, that's why I'm here. This isn't a social call."

Lucy clapped her hand to her mouth. "Oh my God! What's happened? Have you found him?"

"No, no it's not that," said Jo, quickly placing a reassuring hand on her shoulder, "but it is about Rupert. I'm really sorry, but I need to ask to see his guns and the paperwork that goes with them. It's not you in particular, Lucy. I'm checking all the people with licences in the village."

"Oh okay," said Lucy, the colour slowly returning to her face, "come on in."

Jo followed Lucy through the kitchen and down various corridors and hallways. The place was like a rabbit warren. Finally, they arrived in the gun room. It had a low wooden bench and coat hooks running along two walls. There was a door to the outside and a heavy, metal door with bolts in the middle of one wall. One corner had been partitioned off with crates for Tilly and her puppies, who greeted them noisily.

"We thought this made a better home for them, than the master bedroom," explained Lucy.

"That reminds me," said Jo, "I think I've found a home for your last puppy. The chief constable wants one for his daughter."

"Really?" replied Lucy, looking delighted. "How wonderful. Did you hear that, Tilly? One of your babies is going to the chief constable of the county no less."

The black Labrador thumped her tail in response as Lucy produced a huge bunch of keys from her pocket and began searching through. She finally found the right one and unlocked and unbolted the metal door. With a heave, she pulled it open and gasped. The cupboard was empty.

"They've gone," she said, sounding shocked. Jo looked down at the list in her hand.

"There should be a pair of Purdey shotguns, twelve bore," she read aloud.

"Yes, I know," said Lucy, peering further into the cupboard. "They were a present from his parents for his twenty-first birthday."

"When did you last see them?"

Lucy rested against the doorframe and screwed up her face. "The last time I remember Rupert using them was on the Boxing Day shoot. He was home for Christmas. You know, looking back it was only a few weeks before we started hearing about this new coronavirus. It feels like a lifetime ago, doesn't it?"

"Did he take them back to London with him?" Jo asked. She was more interested in the guns that could have been missing for over a year, than reminiscing right now.

"I don't know," replied Lucy.

Jo looked around the gun room. It was a little shabby, but the doors and windows looked secure enough. "You haven't had a break-in or anything?"

"No and nobody else has a key."

"Okay," said Jo as she began making notes, "well, I'll have to report that they are missing, but as a crime doesn't appear to have been committed and as—" she paused "—well as your husband is the registered owner and he's missing too, it makes things a bit more complicated."

"Doesn't it just," said Lucy as she closed the gun cupboard with a sigh.

Jo followed her back to the kitchen.

"Will you stay for a coffee?" asked Lucy.

"No thanks," replied Jo. "I should go. I still have to visit your mother-in-law."

Lucy pulled a face. "You poor thing. Good luck and thanks for coming today. I'm pleased it was you, Jo."

As Jo drove away from Hartwell Hall, she thought about the missing guns and wondered if Rupert's mother might be able to shed any light on their disappearance. Then she slapped her forehead with her hand. She should have checked with Lucy what the hell she was supposed to call Caroline? Was she Lady Hanley or Lady Caroline? Lucy didn't care if you used her title or not, but Jo had a feeling that Caroline would be straight on the phone to the chief constable if she offended her.

In the end, when Caroline opened the front door of the dower house, Jo decided to keep it simple.

"Hello. I'm checking everyone with a gun licence in the

village. I believe you have two firearms on the property."

Caroline stared at her for a second and Jo wondered if she was slightly deaf or had expected her to use the servants' entrance, but all she said was: "It would have been more courteous to make an appointment, but very well. Come through."

The inside of the dower house was as grand as its owner. The place was crammed full of antiques and oil paintings. A haughty Siamese cat was reclining on the silk rug in the drawing room. It swished its tail and gave Jo a look of disdain as she followed Caroline through into the study. It was a small, wood-panelled room, dominated by a huge antique desk and with a view of the immaculate walled garden. The gun cupboard was located discreetly in the corner. Jo watched as Caroline entered the security code on the electronic panel.

"1066. Are you a history buff?" she asked.

"It's the date my late husband's family arrived in this country," replied Caroline coolly.

The door glided open to show two guns resting in a polished wooden rack.

"Can I see the paperwork as well, please?" asked Jo.

"You may," said Caroline moving to the large desk and unlocking one of the drawers. She removed the certificate and handed it to Jo, who noted it was in Caroline's name and had been verified by Dr. Robertson and Colonel Marsden.

"Thank you," she said, handing it back. "Are these the only guns you have here?"

"Yes," replied Caroline, locking the desk drawer.

"It's only that I've just been to Hartwell Hall. The two guns belonging to your son are missing. I don't suppose you know what he might have done with them, do you?"

Caroline didn't look remotely surprised by this news. "I'm afraid Rupert had become rather wayward. There really was no accounting for his actions."

"It must be difficult not knowing where he is," ventured Jo.

Caroline stared at her for a moment with her china blue eyes, before inclining her head slightly. "Naturally. Whatever happens, as a mother you never stop loving your children."

"I guess not. Well, thank you very much for your time, Lady Caroline," said Jo, taking a punt, as she headed back towards the front door.

"You are welcome, Sergeant Ormond, and for future reference, officially you may refer to me as the Dowager Lady Hanley or Caroline, Lady Hanley. Lady Caroline implies that I am the daughter of a duke, marquess or earl, which I am not." She paused. "Although most people in Hartwell simply call me Caroline."

As CAROLINE CLOSED the door behind her, Jo decided she had definitely earned a late lunch at the pub. She hadn't eaten anything all day except for the shortbread biscuit she'd nibbled in the chief constable's office. When she walked into the White Hart, she found Jack talking to Rob, the very sexy property developer, who sadly was one of the few men in the village not to hold a gun licence. Jack's face lit up when he saw her.

"Hey, how's my favourite law enforcement officer?" he asked.

"Thirsty," she replied, slipping her sunglasses onto the top of her head. "Can I get a coke with plenty of ice?"

"Coming up. Good first day on the job?"

"Thrilling. I've been checking everyone's gun licences," she replied, then pointed to a pair of old muskets mounted on the wall above the optics. "Have you got a licence for them?"

"No, but they're antiques and they've been decommissioned. The barrels have been welded shut," Jack protested.

"Still needs to be registered, or I'll have to fine you." She took the glass from him. "Thanks, I'll have a ploughman's too. I'm going to sit outside."

As she left the bar, she heard Jack ask Rob, "Do you think she was serious? You don't think she'd really fine me, do you?"

"Sounds like it, mate. If you ask me, you'll be lucky not to get a restraining order too." Rob laughed.

Jo took her drink out into the tiered beer garden, with open views across the moors. She sat down on one of the wooden picnic benches and, shrugging off her jacket, she tilted her face up to the sun. Taking a long drink, she thought about the missing lord and his missing guns. Her first thought was that he may have used them to take his own life, but the reports she'd read had said he'd walked to the village hall, and he wouldn't have been able to take them there with him without someone seeing. It was possible he'd returned home to get them afterwards without anyone noticing of course, but it still didn't explain where he or they were now. And if he wanted to kill himself, why would he need both guns?

Jo wasn't convinced that nobody else could access the gun cupboard either. Lucy was bound to have left that huge bunch of keys lying around somewhere. She seemed so careless and vague, and Jo really wanted to believe it wasn't an act.

"So how have you enjoyed your day bonding with the locals? Do you feel like one of us yet?" Jack asked, interrupting her thoughts and placing her lunch down on the table.

"Totally. I'm even thinking of buying a flat cap," she replied sarcastically.

"Well, someone must think you belong here. Who gave you that?" he asked pointing to the silver pendant on the chain around her neck. She usually kept it hidden beneath her clothes, but she must have dislodged it when she took her jacket off.

"My social worker gave it to me when I turned eighteen. It was the only thing left with me at the hospital except for a note saying my name was Jo," she said. "I'm assuming Rachel has filled you in on that part of my story too."

But Jack didn't reply straight away. He was looking confused. "So, it wasn't a present from the social worker?" he asked after a moment.

Jo rolled her eyes. Her social workers were so overworked, they barely had enough time to see her for more than a couple of minutes, let alone buy her a thoughtful trinket. "No. Why are you so interested?"

Jack rummaged in his pocket and produced a small leather pouch. He opened it and tipped something out into his hand.

"Snap!" he said. Jo leaned forward and stared. Nestled in the palm of his hand was a small silver disc imprinted with the head of a deer surrounded by runic symbols. She carefully turned it over and sure enough on the other side was the image of an oak tree and the same symbols. It was identical to her pendant.

"I don't understand," she said softly. "You've got one too."

"We've all got them. At least all the old families in the village. The Foxtons, Mum's family, Rob's, the Parkins. They're passed from generation to generation. We call them the Hartwell nobles. I used to wear mine around my neck like you, until the chain broke," Jack explained. Jo frowned as she examined her own silver disc, running her finger over every detail she knew by heart. Although she hadn't let it show at the time, she'd felt overwhelmed when Zara, her fourteenth case worker, the one with green hair, had handed over the file containing all her details including the note and disc she'd been left with. It was the first time she'd been able to hold in her hand a link to her past, to where she came from and who she belonged to. As soon as she had been able to afford it, she'd had it bound in silver and attached to a chain. Since that day she'd never taken it off.

"But what are they?" she asked.

Jack plonked himself down next to her and lowered his voice as if he was doing the voice-over for a film trailer. "Our tale begins long ago in the mists of time."

"Just tell me," she groaned. All day she'd been faced with monosyllabic men; now she was stuck with one who had verbal diarrhoea.

"I will, but it's a good story. I want to do it justice."

Jo shook her head. The man was impossible. She began picking at her ploughman's as Jack cleared his throat and continued.

"Hartwell began life as a Celtic settlement, whose inhabitants were part of the mighty Brigantes tribe. Their Druid priests believed it was a sacred site because of the presence of the well, oak trees, and limestone caves nearby. It was declared that should anyone ever desecrate Hartwell, then they and their descendants shall be cursed forever."

Jo arched an eyebrow at Jack. "A Druid's curse? Seriously? You sound like the evil old bag in the shop."

"Do you want to hear the rest of the story or not?"

Jo held up her hands. "Okay, okay carry on."

Jack lowered his voice again. "After the Norman conquest, King William gave Hartwell to the ancestors of the Hanley family. They tore down ancient oaks to build what is now Hartwell Hall. But as time passed, none of the lords of the manor ever lived beyond fifty—many died horrible deaths or descended into madness. The village was rife with talk of the curse. Then in the reign of—" he paused and wrinkled his forehead "—actually I forget who, one of the Edwards, the second or third maybe, the lady of the manor decided to take action to save her husband and eldest son. She ordered the Hartwell nobles to be made in gold and had them blessed by both a Christian and a Druid priest. Then she gave them to all the old village families who were descendants of the Celts in compensation for destroying the oak trees. She also declared, in a PR master stroke of the time, that it would forever be a link to Hartwell, and should they ever lose their way it would help guide them home. And now you're here. It must be fate."

"If these coins have been around for hundreds of years, they could have ended up anywhere. For all I know, the person who left it with me could have stolen it. And as for a curse on the Hanley family, that's just superstitious crap."

"Maybe it is," replied Jack with a shrug, "but there are plenty around here who believe in it, and Rupert disappearing got them all talking again."

"I thought these, what did you call them? Hartwell nobles? I thought they'd lifted the curse. And I thought you said they were supposed to be gold. Ours are silver."

"Ah, well there's the twist in the tale. You see when the lord found out his wife was planning on giving all that gold to a bunch of peasants, he had a word with the coin maker. He got him to make them in silver but covered in a thin layer of gold. Eventually, the gold wore off, the villagers felt cheated and that's why they say the curse was never really lifted. It's also why the male members of the Hanley family have always had a reputation for being unscrupulous."

Jo took a sip of her drink. She didn't believe in fate or that she belonged in this village, but she'd been thinking, and it might actually be her route back to London. If she found out what had happened to the missing Lord Hanley, it could convince her old boss that she should be back in the Met.

"What's your take on Rupert? Were the two of you friends?" she asked.

Jack's jovial smile faded, and his face clouded before he

replied, "No, I wouldn't say we were friends exactly. We used to hang around together a bit when we were kids. Me, him, Rachel, and Rob used to play in the old Druid caves— you know, just on the edge of the moors?"

Jo shook her head. She hadn't ventured out on to the moors yet.

"Well anyway, he was sent to boarding school when he was eight. After school he went to uni and I was busy with rugby. But it wasn't only a timing thing, he changed. He got quite arrogant and would drink too much. Not to have a good time, but to get totally out of it. Then he started with other stuff too." He paused for a second and shook his head. "When he was home Guy would meet him for a drink now and then, and Max was always around sucking up to him, but I wouldn't say he had any friends round here. Sad really. We all thought he might settle down when he married Lucy and focus on running the estate. He did for a couple of years, then Freddie came along, and he started buggering off to London for weeks at a time, getting up to his old habits again."

"When did you last see him?" asked Jo trying her best to sound casual and not like a police officer. Jack raised an eyebrow.

"Shouldn't you be shining a light in my face or something, DS Ormond?"

Jo gave a wry smile; she'd clearly failed. "I'm just interested, and you must think it would be better for Lucy and Freddie to know where he is."

Jack studied her for a minute. His dark eyes, usually so full of humour, were now serious.

"Okay, it was the night he disappeared. It was that Friday in March when all the pubs and restaurants were told they'd have to close. The place was packed. We all knew a full lockdown was on the way. I assumed Rupert had come home to be with Lucy and Freddie, but actually I think he was more interested on what was happening at that night's parish council meeting. They were due to decide whether some land he wanted to sell to Rob could be built on. He was in here bending the colonel's ear, trying to find out beforehand which way the decision would go."

At that moment, Reverend Davenport popped his head out of the pub's back door. "Oh, there you are, Jack! Shall I help myself if you're busy?"

"I'll be right with you, Rev," Jack called over, then lowering his voice so only Jo could hear: "I'd better go, or he'll be pouring himself triples and drinking all my profits."

He hauled himself to his feet and Jo watched him as he walked away.

"Was it granted? The planning permission?" she called out.

Jack looked back; his expression serious again. "Yes, Rob went ahead and bought it from the estate." He paused. "Look, we all told the police everything we knew at the time. Lucy's had it tough. Please don't go dragging it all up again. Let sleeping dogs lie."

Then he disappeared into the pub. Jo frowned as she took a bite of pork pie. She was sure that at least one villager hadn't told the police everything and that was the second time today a man had asked her not to upset Lucy.

AFTER HER LATE lunch, Jo left the pub and made her way back to her cottage. She could enter the details of the gun licence checks online and email them back to headquarters while working on her tan in the garden. As she walked home, a Golf GTI sped by, its engine revving loudly. It had Bradford plates and a broken rear light, and the driver was a young South Asian guy. It pulled up outside the shop and the driver got out and went inside. Jo shook her head. The poor sod was bound to get the third degree from Nora, who was deeply suspicious of anyone who wasn't local.

An hour or so later, Jo—who had been basking in the sun—heard Meera's front door slam. Hurriedly she stubbed her cigarette out against the wall and began wafting her hands to get rid of the smoke. When it came to fags, the woman was better than a sniffer dog. Jo suddenly stopped wafting. What Meera wasn't, though, was a door slammer. She was the calmest, most controlled person Jo had ever met. She stood up and listened. There were raised voices coming from next door. One of the voices was definitely male. Jo placed her hands on top of the stone dividing wall and hauled herself up. She swung her legs over and landed softly next to the climbing roses. She crept towards her neighbour's house.

Peering in through the kitchen window, she could see Meera in the sitting room arguing with a man. It was the same man who she'd seen earlier in the Golf. Straining her ears, she could only make out the odd word the man was saying. "Respect", "family", and "disgrace". Suddenly Meera appeared in the kitchen. She was backing away from the man who towered over her.

Jo had seen enough. She began hammering on the window with her fist. "Meera!" she shouted. "Are you okay?"

Meera and the man both turned around in surprise and Meera moved to quickly open the back door for her.

"Oh hello, Jo, how are you?" said Meera attempting to sound normal although her voice was shaking.

"Who the hell are you?" demanded the man.

Jo stepped through the door. "Police," she said. "Who the hell are you?"

"Jo, this is my brother Nishit. Nish, this is my neighbour and friend Detective Sergeant Ormond." Meera still sounded slightly breathless as she spoke, but the stress she placed on the word *neighbour* wasn't missed by her brother. He narrowed his eyes but took a few steps back.

"Right. I'll be going then. Think about what I said, Meera."

He strode out through the sitting room and slammed the front door behind him. Meera sank down on to one of the kitchen chairs.

"What the hell was that all about?" asked Jo.

"He isn't very happy about me moving away," said Meera quietly. "And a friend of his saw me and Krish in Helmsley with Ben. He accused me of having an affair. Demanded I stop or he'd tell Dev."

"You having an affair!" exclaimed Jo, furious on Meera's behalf. "It's Dev who's shacked up with someone, not you. Don't they know that?"

Meera closed her eyes and began massaging her temples.

"Please don't shout, Jo. My head is throbbing, and Nish was just upset."

"You know it's at times like this that you should seriously consider drinking. Why don't you go and lie on the sofa and I'll make you a cuppa?"

"Thank you," replied Meera, getting to her feet and making her way through to the sitting room. Jo looked around the kitchen. It was the same size as her own but was far tidier and much better stocked. She took a guess and opened the cupboard above the gleaming chrome kettle. She was faced with a row of neatly aligned boxes of tea.

"What do you want? Yorkshire, Green, Earl Grey, Darjeeling, or another one I can't pronounce?" she called out.

"Earl Grey will be perfect thank you, with a drop of milk, no sugar, please."

Jo made the tea and carried it through to Meera, who was looking slightly calmer.

"If you want, I can hang around for a bit," she offered, but Meera shook her head as she sipped the tea.

"No, thank you. It's very kind of you, but I'll be fine. Nish won't bother me again now he's said his piece. I'll drink this, then go and collect Krish from school."

"Okay, if you're sure. You know you can always shout if you need me," said Jo. She paused then bent down and self-consciously gave Meera a quick hug. Then she left the way she'd arrived, through the back door and over the wall.

All evening, she kept an ear out for any unusual noises next door but didn't hear anything untoward. She was still angry on Meera's behalf. What sort of a brother barged into his sister's house accusing her of having an affair? He should have been sticking up for her. Meera was one of the kindest people she'd ever met. She'd even filled Jo's freezer with Tupperware boxes of her tandoori lamb and murgh malaiwala.

"It's in case you are on a late shift and the takeaways are all closed. Besides, I enjoy cooking. It reminds me of my mum, but Krish refuses to eat it," she had explained, when Jo had tried to thank her.

Jo frowned to herself. What had Meera done to deserve a brother like Nish, or a husband like Dev, come to think of it? And another thing, why did she need to be reminded of her mum? That was an odd thing to say. Her parents only lived a couple of hours away and Meera's house was full of photos of them, with their arms around their daughter, and yet they hadn't been to visit her once. Come to think of it, there wasn't even a "Welcome to Your New Home" card on display. Surely that was the sort of thing parents would send their daughter. It was very weird.

Jo closed her eyes and as she drifted off to sleep in front of the ten o'clock news, she thought that it was at times like this she was lucky not to have a family.

CHAPTER EIGHT

"WHERE'S MUM?" ASKED Rachel. She was less than happy to find her sister already sitting at the farmhouse kitchen table. It was lunchtime and she'd hurried over from work to see how Mary was today. She'd been worrying about her mother more and more recently. She'd organised various aunts, uncles, and cousins to call in and check on Mary while she was teaching, and she'd asked one of the electricians who worked for Rob to fit a smoke alarm in the kitchen. But still she was constantly checking her phone in case one of the farmhands had called to report another near miss or lucky escape.

"Upstairs looking for Jenny's worming tablets," replied Becky as she slipped the booklet that had been on the table in front of her, back into her bag on the floor.

"Why aren't they in the medicine cupboard?" asked Rachel moving towards a wall cupboard to the left of the sink. They all knew the bottom shelf was for any medical treatments or remedies for the farm animals, middle shelf for the dogs and cats, and the top shelf reserved for humans. She opened the cupboard to check for herself, but there were no worming tablets in sight.

"Oh, you know what she's like these days. She's always

losing stuff," replied her sister airily. Rachel closed the cupboard door, then swiftly bent down and retrieved the booklet, swatting Becky's hand away as she protested.

"Hey! That's mine!"

"What is this? More crap about holiday cottages? I told you she isn't up to having strangers here."

Rachel looked down at the glossy A5-size brochure in her hand. However, it wasn't about converting farm buildings. It was a prospectus for St Chad's Prep School in Harrogate. A collection of smiling children in immaculate uniforms with crest blazers beamed up at her from the cover.

"Are you thinking of sending Araminta here?"

"Maybe," replied Becky. "Max says you can't put a price on education."

Rachel flicked straight to the back page and gave a low whistle. "Well clearly you can. It's over five grand a term. Have you two won the lottery or something?"

"You know it's actually very common to talk about money, Rachel," Becky replied, sounding so pompous, Rachel knew she must be parroting another one of Max's lines. She narrowed her eyes, but her sister didn't meet her gaze.

"I hope you aren't here asking Mum to pay."

"What if I am discussing it with her? She likes to help out and it's up to her what she does with her money."

Rachel could feel a wave of anger rising inside her.

"That money was meant to look after her and Dad in their old age. She's on her own now and you know her memory isn't great. If she ever needs to go into a home for specialist care, we'll be looking at five grand a week, not a term. She can't afford to waste it."

Becky tossed her ponytail and pouted.

"Don't be so melodramatic, Rachel. Besides we're only looking, but it wouldn't be a waste. A place like St Chad's could open all sorts of doors for Minty. As Max always says it's not what you know, it's who you know."

"She's four years old!"

"Yes, she is, but she's also Mum's only grandchild. Let's face it, you certainly won't be providing her with any."

Rachel put the brochure down and looked at her sister coldly. "What is that supposed to mean?"

Becky slipped the brochure back in her bag and folded her arms. "You know exactly what I mean. I might not have been to university like you, but even I know you need a man to make a baby."

Rachel's face flushed red. "The last thing I want or need is a man in my life, especially one as pathetic as Max," she spat out. Becky jumped to her feet.

"No, you're far too busy mooning over Lucinda Hanley. God, it's so embarrassing. You're the pathetic one. Pathetic and disgusting."

Rachel raised her hand and there was a loud crack as it made contact with Becky's cheek. Becky shrieked and sprang back clutching her face.

"You slapped me!" she howled in outrage. Mary and Jenny the dog both came running into the kitchen at the sound of all the commotion. Becky immediately burst into noisy tears.

"What on earth's going on?" asked Mary, hurrying over to comfort Becky, while Rachel stood with clenched fists, shaking in fury.

"She hit me!" Becky blubbed.

Mary put her arm around her younger daughter and turned to Rachel. "Oh dear, that wasn't very kind, Rachel," she said. "Don't you think you should apologise to your sister?"

"No, Mum, I don't. She had it coming," Rachel replied, before turning on her heel and marching out of the kitchen, not trusting herself to say anything more. As usual in times of stress, she headed straight to the stables. Her hands were still shaking as she slid the bolt back. Bailey gave a little whinny when he saw her. She stepped inside and leaned back against the cool stone wall, resting her hand on her old friend.

How the hell did her stupid sister know how she felt about Lucy? Did everyone know? She thought she'd been so discreet. Bailey nudged her with his nose, and she gently scratched his ears, scrunching her eyes closed against the sting of tears. Although she hated the thought of the rest of the village laughing at her, it was the jibe about not having children that had really stung her. Not because she thought Becky was right, and quite honestly after spending the morning teaching Jared Parkin, she wasn't sure she wanted children, but it had reminded her of when she'd told her parents she was gay.

It was only a few days before she was due to leave for university. She hadn't slept a wink the night before, trying to come up with the right words that wouldn't shock them. In the end, the words had come tumbling out in a jumble as the three of them sat round the kitchen table drinking tea. Her parents had exchanged a quick glance, then her dad had shrugged and said, "I thought as much. You're the only girl in the village not batting her eyelashes at Rupert Hanley."

"We're happy as long as you're happy," her mother had assured her as she wrapped her arms around her, and Rachel's shoulders had sagged with relief. "But it's such a shame you won't have a family."

"Don't be daft, Mary," her dad had replied briskly. "If she wants children, she can go to one of them clinics. She can get artificially inseminated like we do with our best ewes."

"Dad!" Rachel had pleaded in embarrassment, but not able to stop herself laughing.

Her dad had grinned back at her across the table. "Just make sure you pick a prize ram. Preferably a tall one, otherwise your kids might end up with short little legs like you and your mother," he teased.

Rachel closed her eyes and wrapped her arms around Bailey's neck. She would give anything for her dad to be back with them. She missed him so much. His calmness, his sense of humour, his no-nonsense attitude. Everything. Taking a deep breath to compose herself, she gave Bailey a last kiss. She would love nothing more than to saddle him up, ride out across the moors, and leave everything behind. Unfortunately, duty called and besides, the poor old thing had been limping recently. Reluctantly, she made her way out of the stables and back to school in time for afternoon lessons.

THE GOING-HOME BELL had rung ten minutes ago. The other children had all been collected, but there was still no sign of Lucy. Rachel stood with Freddie in the playground. They were half-heartedly playing a game of I-spy as they waited for her to turn up. Rachel had tried calling her, but her phone was engaged. Finally, they spotted Lucy's Discovery chugging around the corner. It was splattered with mud as usual and the radiator grille was dented from when she'd hit one of the stone troughs outside the pub, while trying to avoid a pheasant.

Rachel experienced the odd sensation not looking forward to seeing her. Instead of her heart leaping, it sank. Since her altercation with Becky at lunchtime, the thought of others knowing what she thought had been her secret, made her feel more and more uncomfortable as the day wore on.

Lucy's car bumped up on to the cobbles outside the school gates and she jumped out. She must have finally been to the salon, because her hair was looking glossier than ever and her eyes were sparkling, the way they did when she was excited about something.

"Hello, you two. Sorry I'm late again. I've been on the phone all afternoon to all sorts of exciting people: wedding planners and event co-ordinators and location scouts," she gushed.

"You took Jo and Meera's advice then," said Rachel, sounding calmer than she felt.

"Yep, and they all sounded really keen. I'm thinking of holding a reception or something and inviting as many as possible," Lucy chattered on as she produced a couple of pound coins from her pocket and handed them to Freddie.

"Would you like to get a treat, darling?"

"Thanks, Mum." The little boy's face lit up as he took the money and ran down the street to the shop.

Lucy watched him go then turned back to Rachel. "The thing is, the place is such a wreck, I'm going to need to tart it up a bit before I invite anyone around."

"Really? I thought shabby chic was all the rage?"

Lucy smiled and as usual Rachel's heart flipped.

"We went past shabby chic about six months ago. We're currently at the dilapidated decay stage, and I'm not sure that's ever been fashionable." She paused as she began to chew her lip and then looked down at her feet. "I was thinking of asking Rob Harrison if he could help, but I don't know him that well, and you're good friends with him so..." She trailed off.

Rachel started shaking her head as her stomach contracted. "We used to hang around together when we were kids, but I wouldn't say we were good friends," she said, struggling to keep her tone neutral.

Lucy frowned. "I would talk to him myself, but I always seem a bit flustered whenever he's around." She paused and tucked her hair behind her ear. "Erm, is it true he was in prison?"

Rachel gave a tight smile. After the day she'd had, she really couldn't handle hearing Lucy tell her about feeling flustered around Rob Harrison. "Yes, something happened when he moved to Leeds, and he went to prison for a while, but he's never spoken to me about it. I really think it would be better if you spoke to him yourself."

Lucy looked disappointed and Rachel realised it was

probably the first time she'd ever refused her something. At that moment Freddie returned with his sweets.

"Okay then, I'll see you later, Rach," Lucy said.

"Bye, Miss Foxton," called Freddie as he climbed into the car.

Rachel stood and watched them disappear into the distance. With a sigh, she turned away and found she was face to face with Caroline.

"Good afternoon, Rachel."

"Hello, Caroline," replied Rachel, warily. When she was a little girl, she'd always found Caroline slightly terrifying, and even now as a grown woman, that feeling hadn't entirely left her.

"How's your mother? I hear she's been rather forgetful of late."

Rachel pursed her lips. No doubt it was Max she'd heard this from. She hated the thought of him gossiping about her mother.

"She's fine, thank you, Caroline. Since she lost Dad, she's had a little trouble sleeping, so she's very tired. Nothing more."

"Good, well as long as she's still compos mentis and not talking nonsense. Tell her I'll drop by and see her soon."

Before Rachel could reply, Caroline turned and crossed the road back to the dower house. Rachel frowned. She'd never considered her mother and Caroline to be close, but she hoped what she'd told her was right and that her mother was tired and nothing more. She began walking towards her cottage, but really didn't feel like being alone with her thoughts all evening; instead, she headed into the White

Hart. She ordered a large glass of red from Shirley, carried it out to the beer garden, and found a quiet table with a view out across the moors.

Rob and some of the guys he worked with were at another table. She leaned back in her chair, closed her eyes and listened as Jack regaled them with one of his rugby stories. It was the one about how he got chased by an emu while on a tour of Australia. Rachel could remember him telling her and Lucy the same story. Lucy had laughed so much she'd cried. Rachel felt tears begin to well up in her own eyes. There was a roar of laughter as Jack delivered his punchline. Bloody Rob Harrison, who'd had women falling at his feet since he was a teenager, now had Lucy feeling flustered. A tear trickled down her cheek and a shadow fell across her face. She opened her eyes to see Jack standing over her, looking concerned.

"You all right, Rach? It's not like you to drink alone."

Another tear slipped down her face, and she quickly brushed it away. "I'm fine, just feeling sorry for myself."

Jack sat down, put his arm round her and hugged her tight. Rachel leaned into her old friend and rested her head on his shoulder.

"You know they wouldn't call it a crush if it didn't hurt, would they?" he said quietly.

Rachel tilted her head to look at him. "How did you know?"

"It's kind of difficult to miss the way your face lights up whenever you're with her."

"Becky guessed too."

"Yeh, she was in here at lunchtime. I saw the bruise."

"She's such a drama queen." Rachel paused and sniffed. "Do you think Lucy knows?"

Jack shook his head and handed her his large white handkerchief. "No. I like Lucy a lot, but if you look up clueless in the dictionary, you'll find a picture of her there."

"I'm the one who's clueless. I'm an idiot for wasting all this time on someone who'll never feel the same about me."

"You're not an idiot, but you've been stuck in Hartwell too long. The place isn't exactly teeming with attractive young women. Trust me I can vouch for that."

Rachel blew her nose and smiled. "You're a fine one to be giving advice. You're just as bad with Jo."

"True, but at least I'm in the right fifty per cent of the population that she's attracted to. I'm actually beginning to look forward to another pandemic, then I might get to be the last man on earth."

Rachel jabbed him with her elbow. "Oh, shut up," she said with a laugh. "Seriously, what do you think I should do?"

Jack smiled and shrugged his massive shoulders. "Do what I do. Keep plodding on and make the best of things. One day, we'll look back at all this and laugh."

"Promise?"

"Promise."

CHAPTER NINE

I T WAS FRIDAY night and Lucy arrived at the White Hart just as the quiz was about to start. Rachel had talked Jo and Meera into joining their team. She'd always been competitive, and it drove her mad that she and Lucy always came last.

"With you being strong on sport, Jo, and Meera's medical knowledge and reading so much, we might actually win for once," she said confidently as the four of them took their seats at the table in the window.

Half an hour into the quiz and the other three were huddled together conferring, but Lucy had yet to answer a question. Bored, she looked around at the other tables and noticed Rob sitting with Dan and Ben as usual. She watched as he picked up his phone from the table and motioned to the others that he was going outside to take a call.

"I'll go get another round in," she whispered and slipped behind Jack and through into the snug. Guy was there chatting to Shirley, who always took over the bar while Jack acted as compere.

"Hi, Shirley. Please can I have a mineral water, a Stella and two G&Ts."

"Coming right up, love," replied the landlady, who was

now a henna redhead.

"Have you abandoned your team?" asked Guy.

"Not exactly. I doubt the others have even noticed I've gone. It's the literature round, so I thought I'd leave them to it. I honestly can't remember the last time I picked up a book," she said with a shrug, then over Guy's shoulder she spotted Rob outside. "Would you excuse me for a sec, Guy. I'll be back for the drinks, Shirley," she called as she headed to the door. Rob was slipping his phone back into his pocket as Lucy stepped outside. He turned round in surprise when he heard her footsteps.

"Sorry, am I disturbing you?" she asked.

"No, I was just taking a call from my sister. She's out in New Zealand, and with the time difference it can be difficult to talk to her. Did you want to speak to me?"

"Yes, I've got a proposition for you."

Rob raised an eyebrow and grinned. "Okay go ahead. I can't remember the last time I was propositioned."

Lucy felt herself flush, but she wasn't going to be put off. She'd spent the whole afternoon working out her finances and planning which rooms she could show the agents, scouts, and planners she'd invited to view Hartwell Hall.

"Would a thousand pounds be enough to employ two decorators for a week?"

"Yes, more than enough. Why?"

"Well, I was hoping to use your guys, those who did the Hayloft. I'd like them to do some work up at the house, but it would only be superficial stuff: replacing the worst of the rotten woodwork, painting over the damp patches, papering over the cracks, literally," she said, her words tumbling out in a rush, but Rob started shaking his head, his expression serious again.

"That will be a waste of their time and your money," he replied. "It will only last a few months. You need to strip back the plaster and sort the roof and…"

"I know, I know, but this is just to tide me over. A quick fix. I only need it to last a few months. You see, I've got some people coming in a couple of weeks who'll hopefully want to use the place as a film location or somewhere to hold a wedding. I need to impress them, then with all the money I make, I can do the proper work over winter."

Rob stared at her intently with those disturbing blue eyes of his for a moment.

"Okay, when do you want them to start?"

"Monday?" asked Lucy, hopefully.

"You don't ask much, do you? Okay, I'll bring two decorators round first thing Monday and don't worry about any dodgy woodwork—I'll sort that out myself."

Lucy frowned and began chewing her lip. "That's really kind, but I'm not sure I'll be able to afford you too," she said hoping he wasn't going to take offence, but he just grinned.

"I don't want paying, but I want you to promise me that when you've made your money, you'll let my guys give you a price for the serious work and not those chancers Max found."

"Deal," replied Lucy holding out her hand. Rob took it and held her gaze for a moment.

"Deal," he echoed. Lucy smiled and then from inside the pub there came the sound of cheering. She turned and peered through the window. It looked like her team had won without her.

ON MONDAY AFTERNOON, Lucy was in the butler's pantry cleaning the champagne flutes for the visitors and wondering if she should serve prosecco or raid the hall's wine cellars for the real thing. Next door in the dining room, Rob was replacing the pieces of skirting board that were so damp they had actually begun sprouting fungus. She could hear his saw and hammer at work while Freddie chatted away to him. Her little boy was home early after a school trip to York. He had been shy and a little apprehensive when he saw the workmen at first, but then curiosity had got the better of him and now they couldn't shut him up.

"Are those magic mushrooms, Rob?"

"Definitely not. Who told you about magic mushrooms anyway?"

"Jared was talking about them on the bus on the way back from the Viking Museum."

"Was he now?"

"Yes. Rachel, I mean Miss Foxton, told him to be quiet," replied Freddie seriously, "Did you know that in the Jurassic era some dinosaurs ate fungus that made them hallucinate?"

"I would not want to meet a hallucinating T-Rex."

Freddie laughed. "No, it was the plant eaters who ate the fungus."

"Ah well yes, that would make more sense."

"You could be a plant eater. You're tall with long arms and legs."

"No, I'd have to be a meat eater. I like steak and burgers too much."

"I like burgers and sausages, but Mum always burns them," said Freddie seriously. Rob laughed and in the butler's pantry, Lucy, shook her head ruefully. Nobody could ever accuse her son of not being honest.

"So, what dinosaur would you be then?" she heard Rob ask.

"I used to want to be a triceratops, but now I think I'd like to be a pterodactyl—they're actually flying reptiles not dinosaurs. They could hang upside down in trees."

"Impressive. I tell you what. If you go and find where I left my tape measure, I'll fix you up a rope swing out on that old horse chestnut tree in your garden, then you can pretend to be a pterodactyl, if your mum doesn't mind that is."

"She won't," said Freddie excitedly as he dashed off on his mission.

Lucy peered round the door of the pantry. "He's not bothering you, is he?" she whispered.

Rob turned around and smiled. "Not at all—he's good company."

"I think so," she agreed, "but then I'm biased. How are you getting on?"

"Fine, we'll easily be done in time."

"That's wonderful! I'd better keep refuelling you with tea." She walked over and reached down to pick up his empty mug. As she did, he noticed the ugly red scar on her wrist. She'd removed the bangles that normally covered it, in case they knocked against the champagne flutes.

"That looks nasty," he said looking up at her with concern.

"I've always been clumsy," she said quickly pulling down

her sleeve. She turned to go.

"Are you nervous about all the people coming here?" he asked, his tone serious.

She paused and thought for a second, then shook her head. "Not really—I like meeting new people and besides Max will be here. He'll probably handle most of the business side of things."

Rob raised an eyebrow. "Does he know as much about event planning and producing films as he does about building maintenance?"

"Well, I don't know much either."

"Maybe not, but in my opinion, your visitors would rather talk to the organ grinder than the monkey."

"That's not very kind."

"Okay then the lady of the house not her agent."

"You really don't like Max much, do you?"

"I think he's a jumped-up fake, but that's not the point. If I was going to recommend a place, put it on my website or in my brochure, or whatever, I would want to speak to the owner not someone with a naff navy blazer and a fake accent who works for her."

"To hear you talk, anyone would wonder why I would employ him at all."

"They'd be right," said Rob as Freddie reappeared, proudly holding the tape measure.

CHAPTER TEN

"NOT TOO HIGH, Krish!" Meera called out as her son flew through the air on the new rope swing. She was sitting with Jo and Rachel out on the terrace at Hartwell Hall, basking in the warmth of the early evening sun. Bees and butterflies hovered around the formal lavender and rose beds while water tinkled and splashed out of the ornate fountain in the middle of the glistening pond. Lucy had invited them around for supper, to celebrate winning the pub quiz and to see the work she'd had done. Freddie and Krish were playing on the edge of the lawn.

Rob had done better than simply make a rope swing. He'd also spent an afternoon building a wooden platform complete with safety rails and ladder in the tree. Now the two boys had turned it into a Viking fort and were brandishing the wooden swords recently purchased on the school trip to the museum in York. From the sound of their laughter, they were having a wonderful time. Their shouts and shrieks only interrupted by the occasional shout of "Do be careful!" from Meera. She had been slightly anxious about the height of the platform, but at least she could relax knowing Krish was away from the tumbleweeds of dog hair that seemed to collect and drift through every room of Lucy's home.

"How was the trip to the museum, Rachel?" asked Meera, still keeping one eye on her son. "Krish hasn't stopped talking about it."

"Put it this way, the first thing I did when I got home was pour myself a very large G&T," replied Rachel. "On the way back, Jared thought it would be a good idea to shove rune stones up his nose."

"Yuck!" replied Lucy wrinkling her face in disgust. "Anyone else have any news? Has Jack won you round yet, Jo?"

Jo smiled but shook her head. "No. I keep telling you—he's not my type."

"That's a shame. A romance would be nice." Meera sighed.

Jo twisted round in her seat to look at her. "What about you and Ben?" she asked. "He's been spending a lot of time at your place. Whenever I come home, his car's parked outside."

"He's just a friend," replied Meera, "and he's been very kind to Krish."

Jo raised an eyebrow. "Maybe he'd like to be more than friends."

"Don't be silly. Besides I'm a married woman," said Meera primly.

"Only technically," said Rachel. "If Dev can have someone else, why shouldn't you? Or, better still, make a clean break and get divorced."

Meera lowered her sunglasses and folded her arms. "I promised Dev I wouldn't seek a divorce. His family in India would be very upset, as would mine. We are living separate lives; things are perfectly fine as they are," Meera insisted.

"It hardly seems very fair on you," persisted Rachel.

Lucy had been listening and nodding as she'd struggled to open a bottle of wine for several minutes. Suddenly the corkscrew fell apart in her hand. "Oh bugger!" she exclaimed. "Why does nothing in this bloody place ever work properly? I'll be back in a second. Don't say anything interesting until I get back," she called out as she disappeared out of the door.

Rachel immediately turned her attention back to Meera. "Doesn't it feel like you're living a lie? How are you ever going to move on with your life?" she asked.

"Hold on a second, Rachel," interrupted Jo. "I don't think you're really in a position to be telling Meera to move on with her life."

"It's okay, Jo," said Meera quickly. She could see where this was heading and wanted to avoid any confrontation between her two friends.

"No, it isn't, Meera," insisted Jo. She pointed to Rachel. "You're never going to move on with your life, while you're still in love with Lucy."

Rachel's cheeks had turned bright red. She turned to Meera. "You know too?" she asked.

"I did wonder," replied Meera gently.

"Are you going to tell Lucy?" she asked, quietly.

"Tell me what?" asked Lucy breezing back in brandishing the now-open bottle of wine.

Meera took in Rachel's stricken face and Jo's folded arms and stubborn expression. She took a deep breath. "That Dev's gay. He didn't leave me for another woman, but for a man."

Three pairs of eyes turned and stared at her.

"What the hell!" gasped Jo.

"Oh my God! When did you find out?" asked Lucy.

"On our wedding night. It wasn't a success and he slept on the sofa in our hotel suite afterwards," said Meera. Her cheeks began to burn in humiliation at the memory. She'd lain there trembling in anticipation in her new cream silk negligee. A few minutes of fumbling and uncomfortable thrusting and it was all over. Then Dev had kissed her on the cheek, told her he would sleep on the sofa and wished her a goodnight. Lying alone in that vast hotel bed all night, she'd tried to work out what on earth she'd done wrong.

Then the next morning, a handsome waiter had delivered breakfast to their room. She'd watched the way Dev smiled at him and suddenly she knew. Her husband was never going to look at her that way.

"It was the one and only time we had sex, but miraculously I conceived Krish," she explained, then gave a wry smile. "When I told Dev I was pregnant, I've never seen anyone look so relieved. His ordeal was over."

"Didn't you have any idea before you married him?" asked Lucy.

Meera shook her head. "We didn't actually meet before the wedding. He was living in India. Our parents had arranged it."

She ignored a loud tut from Jo. She was used to this reaction to the idea of an arranged marriage, but plenty of people—including all her cousins—had arranged marriages and were very happy. Hardly any of them were divorced compared to the English couples she knew.

"I believed they were doing what was best for me. They knew Dev's family. His father supplied my father's factory with fabric. Before Dev came over from India, we Skyped each other, and he was everything I could have dreamed of: handsome, charming, funny, educated, a lawyer," said Meera, remembering how proud her father had been to arrange a union with one of the wealthiest families back in his home city.

"Couldn't you, I don't know, get it annulled or something?" asked Jo.

Meera shook her head. "Not after I found out I was pregnant. I wanted a baby very much, so I confronted Dev. At first, he denied it, but then he broke down in tears and told me how difficult it had been for him living in India and having to hide who he truly was. He told me how grateful he was to me, for giving him a way out. I felt sorry for him. So, I agreed we should continue living together and look to the outside world like a married couple. I truly believed Dev would be a good father too."

"But he wasn't," said Lucy, who had come to sit next to Meera.

"No," sighed Meera. "While I was pregnant, he passed his exams to practise law here and got a job and a flat in Manchester. He came home when Krish was born but disappeared back there as soon as his family returned to India, after the celebrations were over. He would visit occasionally, usually to attend some family event, to keep up appearances, but to all intents and purposes, I was a single mother."

"You poor thing," said Lucy.

"Actually, I didn't mind too much. I got into a routine with work and looking after Krish and my parents were thrilled to be grandparents. They both worked so hard and sacrificed so much for me, if I'd told them the man they'd chosen for me was gay, they would have been so hurt and humiliated." She paused before quietly adding, "And maybe, if I'm being honest, I didn't want to admit that the man I married couldn't bear to touch me either."

"Is that why you won't ask him for a divorce?" asked Lucy, gently.

Meera looked at her and gave a small smile. "Actually, I did ask him for a divorce, when I told him I was moving here. I lost so many of my patients during the pandemic, it made me rethink things. I told him I wanted to stop living a lie. To begin with he used emotional blackmail, crying, telling me I would destroy both our families, but when he realised I was still serious, that's when he started to become unpleasant."

"Violent, you mean?" asked Jo, but Meera shook her head.

"Oh no, that's not his style at all. But he told me he would fight for joint custody of Krish and talked about moving back to India. He emailed me a newspaper article about how a British mother hadn't seen her son for three years because his father had taken him to India and refused to bring him back."

"So, he was threatening you?" pressed Jo. "You could report him for that."

"No," Meera insisted, "Dev is far too clever to do anything that might incriminate him. He's like those London lawyers you talk about Jo, a smooth talker. The emails always contained phrases such as 'I thought you might find this interesting' or 'this is similar to a case I have been working on', but I knew what he really meant. He was warning me to keep quiet. Not rock the boat. You see his family is very wealthy, but traditional. His father would disinherit him if he got divorced, never mind if he found out he was gay."

Lucy finally remembered to pour the wine and handed out the glasses. For once Meera didn't refuse.

"Surely, he's bluffing," said Jo with a frown. "It sounds like he's having a great time in Manchester—why would he want to go back to India and make life tough for himself again?"

"He and his lover have split up. The man in question was much younger and I don't think he found being stuck in Dev's apartment for months on end as exciting as being wined and dined in the bars and clubs of Manchester," explained Meera, trying to keep the bitterness out of her voice. "And things have changed in India. Homosexuality is no longer illegal. Perhaps he thinks if he took Krish, he could do as he pleased, with his dutiful wife providing his cover story. I keep telling myself he couldn't do it. I have Krish's passport and I keep it under lock and key, but I still have nightmares about him being snatched from his bed or the playground."

"I'd never let anyone take, Krish," said Rachel, speaking for the first time since Meera had begun her tale. Meera smiled and reached over to give her old friend's hand a squeeze.

"So, you really believe he'd do that?" asked Lucy. "Take

Krish from you?"

"I honestly don't know. The logical part of my brain says he's bluffing and doesn't want to go and live in India, but why would I take the risk? Why antagonise him? If he thinks I'm with Ben or anyone else, he might use it against me. Wouldn't you do anything to protect Freddie?"

Lucy nodded silently, as she took a sip of her drink.

"And you haven't had a relationship with anyone else?" asked Jo. Meera looked quite shocked.

"Of course not. I meant my wedding vows even if Dev didn't, and I don't want to attract gossip."

Jo's face creased in concentration. "So, you are seriously telling me you haven't had sex since your wedding night?" she asked incredulously.

"Jo!" exclaimed Lucy. "That's too personal. Besides plenty of conventional marriages go through a dry spell."

"But Krish must be what eight? Nine years old?" protested Jo. "That's not a dry spell. That's a bloody drought! If I were you, Meera, I'd have pounced on Ben by now."

"You don't miss what you've never had," began Meera primly, "so although Ben might be a lovely man—" her voice caught in her throat "—I won't risk losing Krish."

Jo opened her mouth to argue when a high-pitched beeping of a smoke alarm interrupted them.

Lucy leapt to her feet. "Oh bugger! I've forgotten the bloody cottage pie," she gasped, dashing out of the room.

Jo got to her feet wearily. "I'll go and check we don't need the fire brigade." She sighed shaking her head and following Lucy to the kitchen.

Rachel looked up and gave Meera a small smile. "Thank you," she said, quietly.

MEERA CLOSED THE surgery door behind her. The last two patients had cancelled their appointments, so she could leave for the day. The phone in her pocket bleeped. It was half-term and Lucy was looking after Krish for her. She'd sent a text to say she'd finished early and received one back from Lucy saying they were in the garden of the White Hart. Meera pursed her lips. She wasn't sure a pub garden was a suitable place for her son, but at least he would be having fun with Freddie.

She had acted on impulse when she'd told the others the truth about her and Dev. Partly, she'd wanted to spare Rachel, who had looked terrified at the thought of having to confess her feelings for Lucy, but it had actually felt good to be honest. Carrying the secrets, the lies, and the worry around with her all this time had been exhausting. Also, now there were four pairs of eyes looking out for Krish, not just one.

Nish's visit had unsettled her. She'd been naïve thinking she could hide away here. She'd only given her parents her new address, but if her brother could find her so easily, Dev or someone he employed, would have no problem either.

She and her brother had never got on. It was typical of him to jump to conclusions and think the worst of her. Officially, he worked as a delivery driver for their father's factory, but he was forever getting involved with some get-rich-quick scheme. Meera wasn't convinced his business dealings were completely legitimate. No wonder he had disappeared when she'd introduced him to Jo.

As much as she missed her mother and father, she didn't miss Nish much. He had caught her off-guard, but it was the unfairness of the situation—not being able to stand up for herself properly and tell him the truth—that upset her. She had longed to be able to say: *The husband my family chose for me sleeps with other men, so if my son and I want to eat ice cream with a nice, kind vet, it is no concern of yours.* But she didn't. All her life she'd bitten her tongue, done as she was told. Moving to Hartwell had been about taking control and working out what was best for her and Krish.

Her thoughts drifted to Ben. Despite telling the others he was only a friend; she was growing fond of him. He was kind and honest, sometimes a little too honest, but after Dev's sugar-coated, empty words that made a welcome change. She liked his soft Scottish accent and his warm brown eyes that crinkled in the corners. She even liked his slightly chaotic appearance. He reminded her of a mad professor with his hair sticking up and his glasses always skew-whiff. Not that he cared what he looked like—that was nice too.

When she reached the pub's side gate that led into the large, terraced garden, she paused. It looked like a party was taking place. Half the village seemed to be there, and Jack had set up a huge outdoor screen. Then she remembered there was a test match taking place at Headingley. England versus India. One of her patients had mentioned it. An elderly farmer with high blood pressure had asked if he could skip the check-up and just get the repeat prescription, so he could get back home in time for the first ball.

"That really wouldn't be very good for your condition,"

Meera had explained patiently.

"Neither will missing Joe Root bat," he grumbled.

With a pang, Meera thought of her father. He loved cricket. She wondered if he was there in the crowd, cheering on India. It had been his birthday the previous week. She'd sent cards from her and Krish along with a bottle of his favourite whisky and a signed copy of Sachin Tendulkar's autobiography, but when she'd called to wish him a happy birthday, her mother had told her he was out, even though she could hear the theme tune for *Cash in the Attic*—his favourite TV programme—playing in the background. Her mother sent daily texts asking how she and Krish were settling in, but her father still refused to speak to her.

With a sigh, Meera opened the gate and made her way into the garden. The screen was on the upper tier of the garden, with deck chairs and wooden benches for people to sit on and watch the match arranged on the lower tier. There was a white awning over a large table laden with quiches, salads, and pies. Her eyes scanned the crowd. Krish and Freddie lay on their stomachs on the grass, drinking Coke through straws and eating crisps, their eyes fixed on the match. Lucy and Jo were sat next to them at one of the picnic tables. Lucy waved when she saw her and came weaving through the crowd.

"Hi, Meera, how wonderful you finished early," she said kissing Meera's cheek.

"Thank you for taking care of him, Lucy. I'll go and collect him."

"Oh, let him stay a bit longer," said Lucy gently laying her hand on Meera's arm. "It's good for them to have some male company for a change. I know Freddie must be sick of being stuck at home with me so much."

Meera watched Krish cheer along with the others as the opening batsmen hit the ball for six.

"Maybe just for a little while," she agreed.

"Wonderful. I'll get you a mineral water," said Lucy, ducking into the bar.

Meera went to kiss Krish hello, much to his embarrassment, then she took a seat next to Jo who was frowning at her glass of Pimm's as she tried to fish out a mint leaf.

"I should never have let Lucy get the drinks," she grumbled. "It's like trying to down a sodding fruit salad."

"Do you think your dad will be watching?" Meera heard Jack ask Krish.

"I don't know," replied Krish "Grandad and Uncle Nish definitely will be. Dad and his friend like football, but I'm not a big football fan."

"Dad's friend?" queried Jo, under her breath.

"The man who moved in with Dev," whispered back Meera. "Krish saw him once in the background when Dev Skyped him. He said it was his friend. I'm not going to be the one to tell Krish differently."

"It's your call," replied Jo, "but speaking as someone whose entire background is a secret, I don't think he'll thank you."

"Football is rubbish," declared Jack loudly as he handed out beers. "For a real sport you need funny-shaped balls."

This comment caused the two boys to burst into hysterical laughter. Jack was very popular with them as he could be relied on to not only supply the Coke and crisps, but also for an endless stream of jokes that contained what they thought were rude words.

"I think you've finally found your audience," said Jo with a grin as she removed a piece of cucumber from her glass.

"He's always been very good with children," said Shirley giving her a wink, as she passed by with another tray of drinks. "And did I tell you what a good cook he is?" she called over her shoulder. "His beef wellington is out of this world."

"She's even less subtle than my mother." Meera laughed. "She tries to convince every mother with an eligible daughter that Nish is a misunderstood genius with many hidden talents."

"And is he?" asked Lucy, sitting down with them and handing a mineral water to Meera.

"His only talents are drinking too much, gambling too much, and listening to Bhangra music too loudly," replied Meera.

She looked around her. Colonel Marsden was standing beneath the awning, loudly explaining what was wrong with England's batting order as Max nodded obediently next to him. Becky and her little girl were dressed in identical tennis whites, which might explain why Rachel was nowhere to be seen. Rob was positioning one of the large striped parasols over Reverend Davenport who had fallen asleep in a deck chair and was snoring loudly as he slowly turned the colour of a boiled lobster. Nora appeared, complaining loudly that nobody was buying her ready-made sandwiches because the pub was giving away free food and Jack tried to mollify her with a glass of Pimm's. Living in Hartwell, these would be

Krish's childhood memories—so different to her own.

All social gatherings had taken place at the houses of other Indian families. She called everyone auntie and uncle even if they weren't related. There was always far too much food, the hostess terrified that anyone's plate should become empty for a second. Meera would always be dressed in her best clothes and the aunties would coo over her pretty face and glossy hair. At least one uncle thought he could sing and would do so as loudly as possible, while the aunties gossiped about their neighbours. She wondered what they would make of the inhabitants of Hartwell.

Krish had missed out on those gatherings—Meera had avoided them more and more over the years. She'd grown tired of having to make excuses for Dev's absence and the endless enquiries about when she would be producing a little brother or sister for Krish.

MEERA AND KRISH finally left the White Hart's garden when the match stopped for tea. They turned the corner of their lane to find a visitor waiting for them. Ben was standing on their doorstep, his glasses slightly crooked and his hair sticking up as usual. This evening, however, he was also holding a rectangular cardboard box in his hands. Krish rushed to greet him.

"There you are. I hoped I'd catch you," he said.

"Hi, Ben, what's in the box?" asked Krish.

"A surprise for you," replied Ben with a grin.

Meera opened the door and then left the two of them

sitting together on the sofa with the box. She assumed Ben had brought the bat back to be released in their garden. She went into the kitchen, listening to her son's excited squeal as she switched on the oven. She was about to open the fridge when something small and furry shot through from the sitting room, straight past her and up the stairs. Meera squealed in horror and leapt onto a chair. Ben and Krish appeared a second later.

"Don't worry, he won't hurt you," said Ben, as Krish dashed upstairs after the creature.

"Why have you brought a rat into my house?" demanded Meera, furiously.

"It's not a rat. It's a ferret," replied Ben, stepping forward and offering her his hand, but Meera wasn't in the mood to accept assistance.

"Then why have you brought a ferret into my house?"

"It's a present for Krish."

"But you know about his allergies. How could you be so irresponsible?"

"No, no you don't understand," protested Ben. "That's the thing—ferrets have different fur to cats and dogs, so they won't trigger his allergies. It seemed such a shame that someone who loves animals as much as Krish couldn't have a pet, so I did some research and loads of asthmatics have ferrets and I know this farmer in Thirsk who breeds them so…" He trailed off as Krish reappeared cuddling the ferret.

"Isn't he cute, Mum? I'm going to call him Darwin."

"Please put him down, Krish," replied Meera.

"Why? And why are you still standing on the chair?"

Realising she must look ridiculous, she stepped down

with a wobble, which made her even more angry.

"I'm sorry if you're upset," Ben said calmly. "I thought it would be a nice surprise."

"You should have discussed it with me."

"You would have said no."

This was true.

"Then you should have respected my wishes. I know what is best for my son."

"I'm sure that's true about ninety to ninety-five per cent of the time," agreed Ben.

"What do you mean?" Meera demanded.

Ben shrugged his shoulders. "Well, if you want my honest opinion, when it comes to Krish, sometimes I think you are in danger of becoming like one of those silly ladies you see in cities, who carry their dogs around in their handbags."

"Are you comparing my son to a dog?" Her voice rose in indignation. Who on earth did this man think he was?

"It's not an insult. I think boys and dogs are very similar—they both need company, exercise, stimulation. They need to run free. Not be mollycoddled."

"Mollycoddled!"

"Yes, it means…"

"I know what it means," snapped Meera. She could feel herself getting angrier and angrier. To make matters worse Ben was perfectly calm and using the sort of voice she used herself when she was telling patients that an inflamed appendix would not sort itself out and yes, they would definitely need an operation.

Krish stood at the bottom of the stairs, clutching the ferret and watching them both opened-mouthed. His eyes darted between them like they were tennis players in the middle of a long rally. Meera hardly ever raised her voice.

"Please can I keep him, Mum?" he pleaded. "My breathing feels fine."

Meera tried to compose herself. "Is it house-trained?"

"They are very clean," replied Ben grinning at Krish. "I've got a cage and food for him."

"You didn't really answer my question," argued Meera, as Ben disappeared out to his car, returning a second later with all sorts of ferret-related paraphernalia.

"I bought you a present too," said Ben, handing her a DVD of *Jane Eyre*.

"That's one of her favourites," said Krish with a grin.

Meera smiled tightly. "That's kind, thank you," she said. Yet again, it seemed she was outnumbered. So much for taking control of her life—she'd been bamboozled into letting some sort of rodent into her new home. At that moment, Ben's phone bleeped. He peered at the screen.

"Uh-oh looks like I have to go. I'm on call. One of Frank's cows is having problems calving. I'll see you later."

"You're leaving us with the ferret?" she asked suddenly, panicking. "I know nothing about looking after animals."

"Krish does. You'll be fine. You can always call if you need me," he said and with a cheerful wave he was gone.

AFTER SUPPER, SHE, Krish, and Darwin settled down on the sofa to watch *Jane Eyre*, but Meera found she wasn't enjoying the story of the young governess in the wilds of Yorkshire, as much as usual. She kept thinking about what Ben had said about her mollycoddling Krish. How on earth could he comment on her parenting skill, when he had no children of his own? Perhaps she was a little overprotective, but then Krish had been a poorly baby and now she had his father's threats hanging over her. It crossed her mind that she should have told Ben about Dev, but no, she shouldn't have to justify her actions as a mother.

She settled back and tried to enjoy Jane's first encounter with the brooding Mr Rochester, but she still couldn't concentrate. As if sensing her animosity towards him, Darwin kept trying to sit on Meera's lap, as she edged further and further away.

As the film ended, she didn't know whether to be relieved or irritated that Ben appeared to be correct, and Krish's breathing was absolutely fine. It looked like the ferret was here to stay. She did, however, draw the line at him sleeping in Krish's bed.

"Absolutely not! Put him in his cage and make sure it's locked," she insisted at bedtime. She had enough difficultly sleeping, without worrying about a visit from their new furry friend in the night.

A FEW DAYS later before the party to show off the house as an event space, Meera and Jo were in the library at Hartwell Hall, drinking tea and eating Joan's scones. Meera was quite flattered that Lucy had asked her over to give her opinion on an old tapestry she had found in the attic and hung on the wall to hide a section of peeling wallpaper. The French doors on to the terrace were open, and outside Krish and Freddie were playing in the garden. Ben was due anytime to give the puppies their last injections before they could go to their new homes. Meera had given in to Krish's begging for the chance to play with Freddie and watch Ben at work again. She hadn't spoken to Ben since he'd given Darwin to Krish, but she'd taken a little time to reflect on their conversation and finally conceded he might have a point. She was trying very hard to be more relaxed when it came to her son. She had even found some new antihistamines to help with allergies, so he could play with the puppies before they left. Jo had arrived to collect the puppy Chief Constable Carmichael had reserved.

"It looks perfect!" declared Meera, studying the tapestry with a critical eye.

"Do you really, think so?" Lucy sighed. "Rob and his team have been working miracles, but there is still so much to do."

"When's the big event?" asked Jo through a mouthful of scone.

"The day after tomorrow," replied Jo. "I just hope we'll be ready in time."

A sudden burst of loud barking from Tilly and Pickle announced Ben's arrival.

"Hi, Lucy. Hi, Meera. Jo, what are you doing here?" he asked as he strode in through the French doors.

Jo arched an eyebrow. "Nice to see you too, Ben."

The vet looked a little embarrassed. "Sorry, but I thought you'd be down at the Hayloft—you know Rob's new place.

He and his men started digging to bury some cables and found a body. There's a police car there already."

Before he could say another word, Lucy had sprung to her feet, her cup crashing to the floor.

"Watch Freddie for me, Meera!" she shouted as she ran out of the door. Jo sprinted after her.

Meera turned to Ben and shook her head. "Honestly what's wrong with you?"

"What did I say?" he asked, looking genuinely confused.

"I hope you are better at breaking bad news to your patients' owners. Lucy's husband has been missing for over a year and you breeze in shouting about a body being found."

Ben's hand flew to his mouth. "Oh my God, I didn't think."

"Clearly. Now you go and look after those puppies while I clear up this mess before one of the boys cuts themselves," she said bending down to collect the broken bits of cup.

CHAPTER ELEVEN

"LUCY, DON'T BE an idiot," yelled Jo breathlessly when she caught up with her friend and saw she was about to open the door of her four by four. "You're in no state to drive. We'll take my car."

Lucy didn't reply. She was wearing a stunned expression, but she did as Jo told her. As they headed down the long driveway, Jo's phone beeped. Glancing at the screen, she saw it was a message informing her human remains had been discovered at the Hayloft in Hartwell and that uniform were already attending.

"Better late than never," she muttered to herself as Lucy's pale face continued to stare straight ahead. A few minutes later, they arrived in the village hall car park. There was a police car parked at the Hayloft and Rob and his team of builders were standing in the driveway. Two uniformed police officers were already putting yellow 'do not cross' tape around the area. Rob strode over as soon as he saw them and instinctively put his arm around Lucy who was shaking and growing paler by the second.

Jo nodded at him and ducked under the yellow tape and headed straight to where they had been digging. She dropped to her knees and stared intently down at the partially exposed skeleton. After only a few seconds, she stood up and spoke briefly to the two constables, then she hurried back to Lucy who looked like she might collapse at any minute.

"It's not him," said Jo bluntly.

"Are you sure?" asked Lucy, her voice barely louder than a whisper.

"Positive. I've seen enough skeletons to know that this one has been down there longer than a year—more like a couple of hundred. Uniform think the same. They said forensics are on their way."

"Why forensics if you're sure it's not Rupert?" asked Rob.

"They need to confirm it," explained Jo. She placed a hand on Lucy's arm, but her friend didn't seem to be able to focus on her. Maybe she was in shock, "Look, Lucy," she said as gently as she could, "I'll have to stay here and wait for them to turn up and the archaeologists are coming too, but I really don't think it's a good idea for you to be here."

"It's all right. I'll take her home and make sure she's okay," said Rob as he slowly began to guide Lucy towards his pickup truck. Jo watched as Lucy silently climbed into the cab and they drove away towards Hartwell Hall.

Less than twenty minutes later, the forensics team had confirmed that the body discovered had been buried there several hundred years ago and no sooner had they left than the archaeology team from York university arrived. Jo leaned against her car, making notes for the report she would have to submit. Quite a few villagers, including Reverend Davenport and Nora, had gathered at the edge of the cordon, straining their necks to see what was happening. Jo was being careful not to make eye contact with any of them.

Suddenly, there was a commotion and Nora started complaining loudly, as Rachel—dressed in jodhpurs and T-shirt—pushed her way to the front of the crowd. Jo waved to the uniformed officers to let her through, resulting in more complaints from Nora. Rachel ducked under the tape and hurried towards Jo. Her face was flushed, and she was sweaty and out of breath.

"Dan said you'd found a body," she said her eyes fixed on the hole the archaeologists were huddled over.

"It's not him," said Jo.

Rachel turned to her. "Does Lucy know?"

"Yes, she was down here, but she was pretty shaken up. Rob took her home." She paused as her phone rang; she looked at the screen. It was the chief constable, no doubt wondering where his puppy was. "Sorry, Rach, I'll have to take this."

At that moment, a tall woman with wavy red hair and freckles across her nose looked up. She had already introduced herself to Jo as the head of the team from York university. She made her way over to Rachel and held out her hand.

"Hi, I'm Sarah Stevenson. I'm going to be in charge of the dig. Are you a local?"

"Yes, I'm Rachel Foxton. I'm a teacher at the school here."

"Then I expect you'll know that this place was originally a Celtic settlement. We think we might have found a Druid burial site," she said sounding excited, then nodded towards the crowd of villagers. "I have to say, I wasn't expecting this much interest in such a small place."

"A local man disappeared about a year ago. We all thought it must be him."

Sarah's face fell. "Oh I see. You must all be relieved it wasn't him."

"Yes, I suppose so," replied Rachel quietly.

"Look I was hoping to speak to someone who lives here about all the local legends. Would you like to go for a drink later?"

"Erm yes, okay maybe," replied Rachel, then gave her head a little shake. "Look, I'm sorry, but should really go and check on Lucy. It was nice to meet you."

With that she turned and walked away, pushing her way back through the crowd and snapping. "You can all clear off. It's not him."

Sarah looked disappointed and returned to her group. Standing just within hearing distance, Jo had watched their exchange. The archaeologist was right—Lucy should have been relieved, but if anything, she looked even more worried when she left than when she arrived, almost as worried as Rachel, who seemed totally unaware that she was being hit on.

As she watched Rachel striding across the fields towards Hartwell Hall, it occurred to Jo that if she was ever going to find out what Lucy and Rachel really knew about Rupert's disappearance, then this was the time. She went to tell the uniformed officers that she was returning to headquarters, gave her contact details to Sarah—the archaeologist—then returned to her car and headed back to Lucy's.

As she pulled into the driveway, she saw a concerned-looking Joan step out of the gatehouse front door.

Jo stopped and wound down her window. "I take it you've heard?" she asked.

Joan nodded. "Yes, love. Rob stopped on his way past with Lucy to let us know. What a to-do! Poor Lucy was as white as a sheet! Rob said he would stay with her until I can get up there, and Meera is with Freddie. I just want to go and make sure Caroline doesn't hear it from anyone else. See you later, love."

Jo watched her hurry away as she wound up the window. She couldn't believe that in a village as small as Hartwell, Caroline hadn't already heard about the discovery, but if she had, she certainly hadn't hurried down to the village hall to see if her only son had been found.

She drove on up to the Hall and purposely parked at the front door, away from the kitchen and the fields Rachel would be coming across. She quietly made her way around to the back of the house and stopped by the kitchen window. If she wedged herself next to the drainpipe, she could remain hidden but still see what was happening inside.

Lucy was sitting next to the Aga. It was a warm day, but she had a blanket over her shoulders. She was still very pale. Rob appeared with a glass of what Jo guessed was brandy and handed it to Lucy, who managed a weak smile. Then he knelt down next to her and took her hand. Jo could see his lips move, but she annoyingly couldn't work out what he was saying. Just then, she heard the sound of running feet in the courtyard around the corner. Jo waited a few seconds, then sure enough, Rachel came charging into the kitchen. She stopped suddenly when she saw Rob tenderly holding Lucy's hand.

"Luce, are you okay?" she gasped loud enough for Jo outside to hear. Rob let go of Lucy's hand and stood up. He said something and placed his hand on Lucy's shoulder.

Lucy nodded and gave him a weak smile before he turned and left. Jo took this as her cue. She hurried to the corner of the courtyard, paused until Rob reached his pickup truck and had his back to her, then she stepped through the door and tiptoed towards the kitchen.

"It wasn't him," she heard Lucy say quietly.

"I told you he wasn't there," Rachel replied.

"Don't you think it's time you both told me what's going on?" asked Jo, from the kitchen doorway. Rachel and Lucy both jumped and stared at her.

"What do you mean?" asked Rachel, immediately on the defensive.

Lucy leaned back in her chair and closed her eyes for a second. "Jo's right, Rach. I should tell her what happened that night," she said softly. Jo held her breath. She'd been right. The two of them did know something.

"Luce! You don't have to explain anything. It wasn't him," insisted Rachel.

"No, I want to," said Lucy, her voice unusually serious. "This has gone on too long."

"Then let me make you some sweet tea—you look like you're in shock," said Meera. This time it was Jo who was startled as her neighbour quietly arrived through the other door with the last shards of broken crockery. "Don't worry about Freddie, Lucy. Ben has taken the boys to look for butterflies," continued Meera.

"Thank you, Meera, but I'm fine. The brandy is helping." Lucy gave her a small smile. Then she took a deep breath and turned to look at Jo. "I went to see Rupert after the parish council meeting. Rachel stayed here with Freddie while I drove down to the village hall. We'd watched Boris announce the lockdown and the thought of being cooped up here with him for God knew how long, well I simply couldn't handle it. I went down there to tell him he couldn't stay here and that I wanted a divorce."

"Were things that bad?" asked Jo.

"Those injuries on your medical record. Were they..." Meera let her question gently tail off as Lucy nodded her head.

"What injuries? Did he hit you?" demanded Jo, but Meera raised a finger to her lips to silence her as tears began to roll down Lucy's cheeks.

"He didn't take anything when he was here. It was his way of proving it wasn't an addiction, that he could control it, but it made him incredibly irritable. He'd lash out."

"It was more than lashing out," said Rachel shaking her head. "You're still making excuses for him."

Lucy took another sip of brandy before she continued. "Then before he went to the meeting, he got a call saying it looked like planning permission wouldn't be granted. He was furious. He kicked the coffee table over, but it had a full cafetière on it. Boiling-hot coffee went everywhere, including over Freddie and me."

"So, what happened that night?" pressed Jo, wishing she could have spoken to Lucy without Meera and Rachel being there acting like guard dogs, if she got too close to the truth.

"I was waiting for him. Behind the hedge of the Hayloft.

Rob had just started work on it. They'd dug the foundations for the garage. Rupert was the last to leave; none of the others had seen me. I called out his name. He was surprised to see me. He was in a good mood. The planning had passed after all. He suggested we go for a drink to celebrate before the pubs all closed." She gave her head a little shake. "As if I wanted to drink with him after what he'd done to us. That's when I told him it was all over. He didn't think I meant it. Then I threatened to go to the police about him hitting me. He got angry, really angry, saying such awful things about me." She gave a shudder. "Then he started coming towards me. He was shouting. He raised his hand. I picked up a spade that was leaning against a cement mixer. I told him stay back, to leave me alone. He lunged and I hit him. I hit him on the head with the spade." She looked at Jo with pleading eyes. "It was just to get him away from me, but he stumbled, he fell. His head smacked against the side of the cement mixer. It was such a horrible sound. He landed in the trench. There was blood on his forehead, but he was alive. I swear I heard him groan, but I was so afraid of what he might do. I ran."

Lucy put her head in her hands, and Rachel went to stand behind her, her hand on her shoulder. She took up the story, fixing Jo with a steely gaze.

"Lucy was shaking when she arrived back here. She told me what had happened. She wanted to call an ambulance. I said with the hospitals being so overstretched that the paramedics might bring him straight here if he wasn't badly injured. Then she'd be stuck with him and eventually he'd take his revenge for her sticking up for herself. I said I'd drive down there and see how he was and if it was bad, we'd call an ambulance then. I took Lucy's car. I drove on to the building site, turned the headlights on to full beam, but there was no sign of him. I got out of the car and looked into the trench. Nothing. I went to the village hall, but it was in darkness—nobody was there. So then I phoned the Hart, thinking he might have somehow staggered there, but Jack said he hadn't seen him since before the meeting. The only other person I could think of was Caroline, but she wasn't answering her phone, so I guessed she wasn't home. I drove back here and told Lucy I couldn't find him."

"Then you waited twenty-four hours before reporting him missing," said Jo. She was itching to take notes, but knew if she did, they would clam up.

Lucy nodded. "I kept thinking if he wasn't here, then he must have gone back to London, but of course his club and all the hotels had been forced to close. I knew so little of his life down there. I couldn't think who he might be with, so I called the police, thinking they would have more luck tracking him down. I might not have wanted to be married to him anymore, but I still needed to know he was okay."

"But how would he have got to London without his car?" asked Jo.

"Perhaps he could have called a taxi," suggested Meera.

Jo scowled at her, before turning her attention back to Lucy. "Why didn't you tell the police about arguing with Rupert after the council meeting?"

"Why should she?" said Rachel suddenly flaring up. "Hadn't she suffered enough at his hands? If the police found out she'd rowed with him, hit him, been the last person to see him, they might have accused her, just like you are."

Jo raised her palms. "I'm not accusing anyone, but Lucy seemed convinced it was Rupert they found today, even though you told her you didn't see him."

"When Ben said they'd found a body, well, it felt like too much of a coincidence," said Lucy. "I kept thinking Rachel could have missed him, or maybe he'd crawled into a different trench or ditch or something. Since that night I've come up with so many different scenarios."

Jo shook her head in exasperation. "You do know you could both be charged with withholding evidence."

"Only if the police can prove a crime has been committed," replied Rachel, defiantly. Jo held her gaze. She would bet that Rachel had spent hours reading up on what they might or might not be charged with—unlike Lucy, who still looked lost and bewildered. If this had been a police interview and she was reading a transcript of it, she would have put money on Rachel and Lucy knowing exactly what had happened to Rupert and where he was, but this wasn't a police interview, it was two friends telling her a secret that had burdened them for months.

Now she didn't know what to do. What they'd told her was important. If she took it to the chief constable, he might even let her take over the investigation, but could she do that if it led to Lucy's arrest? Seeing her so frightened and knowing what she'd been through, it was impossible not to feel sorry for her.

Jo gave her head a shake. She needed to get out of here so she could figure out what to do.

"Okay, well, I guess I'm pleased you told me what really

happened and that today was a false alarm," she said. "Look, I've got to get back to Northallerton with that puppy for my boss. I'll see you all later."

She left the kitchen and went to the stables where she found the chief constable's puppy waiting for her in his crate, wagging his tail and whimpering a little. It was only as she picked him up that she realised Meera had followed her outside. Her neighbour's face was serious.

"Jo, what has been said today is just between the four of us. You know because if this was official, then Lucy and Rachel should probably have had a solicitor here. They told you as a friend," said Meera, watching her closely.

Jo shifted uncomfortably. Who would have guessed mind reading was one of Meera's hidden talents?

"Also," continued her neighbour, "if it came to it, I think Lucy could say she acted in self-defence. I would certainly testify about the injuries in her medical record."

"I know that," snapped Jo, defensively, but Meera didn't seem put off.

"I realise how important it is for you to impress your superiors," she continued as Jo carried the crate to her car and put it carefully on the back seat and secured it with a seat belt. "And how much you want to return to London…"

Jo spun around angrily and held up her hand before Meera could say anything else.

"Credit me with some integrity, Meera. I might be many things, but I'm not a grass," she snapped. Then she stomped down to the driver's door, climbed into her car, slapped her foot on the accelerator and roared away down the drive, wishing for the hundredth time that she'd never set foot in Hartwell.

CHAPTER TWELVE

L IKE A CHILL wind picking up autumn leaves, the discovery of the skeleton had started rumours about Rupert's disappearance swirling around the village again. Rachel had been looking forward to getting away. She was due to spend the weekend in Newcastle on a training course, but it had been cancelled at the last minute and now she was stuck in Hartwell again.

She'd woken up early and picked some of the wildflowers that grew at the edge of her garden and made a bouquet of poppies, cowslips, daisies, and foxgloves. Then she took the short walk over to the church. It had been almost two weeks since she'd been to see her father, but she'd been so busy with work, and worrying about her mum. She pushed open the wooden gate and took the stone path that led through the other graves to the shady spot next to an old yew tree. Carefully she laid her flowers next to the tub of blue hyacinths her mother had left there.

"Hello, Dad," she said quietly as she gently wiped her hand over the smooth headstone engraved with his name and dates. She'd lost count of the times she wished she could talk to him about what happened that night with Rupert and Lucy. He'd been alive but shielding so she couldn't see him, and it wasn't the sort of conversation she wanted to have over the phone.

"Hi, Dad, my best friend might have killed her husband, but we don't know because we can't find him, and I daren't say anything to anyone, because aside from you and Mum, she's the person I care about most in the world."

Instead, she told herself that she'd ask his advice when the Covid madness was over, but now it was too late. Just then a noise behind her interrupted her thoughts. She looked over her shoulder. A little way up the path near a wooden bench stood Sarah, the red-haired woman from the dig. She smiled and raised her hand in greeting. Rachel frowned. She'd thought she was alone here. She kissed the tips of her fingers and placed them on top the headstone, then she stepped back and began trudging up the path, until she was level with Sarah.

"Sorry did I disturb you?" said the archaeologist.

Rachel shook her head. "No, it's fine. What brings you here?"

"This chap," replied Sarah, pointing to the gravestone she was stood next to. Rachel bent forward and peered at the worn lettering. *Joseph Baxter Tarrant.*

"Is he a relative of yours?" she asked.

"No, more like my inspiration. When he was alive, he was one of the leading experts on Celts and Druid culture. He was researching the Hartwell nobles when he died here almost thirty years ago. I'm writing a thesis on him, but nobody knows much about his private life. I thought I'd post a picture of his headstone on Instagram, see if it rings any bells with anyone."

"It should. Baxter-Tarrant is a fairly unusual name," reasoned Rachel.

"No Baxter was his middle name. In honour of a wealthy great-uncle, I believe."

Rachel smiled. "You really are an expert."

"I should be. Almost all my work is based on research he published. It's so sad he didn't finish his paper on the Hartwell nobles. Hopefully, I might be able to track down a long-lost relative who can tell me why." She paused and pushed a stray red curl out of her eyes. "Are you on Facebook or Instagram?"

"Facebook, mainly, but I'm trying to take a break from social media. One night in lockdown, I realised I'd wasted two hours looking at posts of dogs on surfboards."

Sarah laughed. "For me it was cats that look like famous people. My favourite was one that looked like Beyoncé, but admittedly that was actually a lion."

"Well, I hope your post gets plenty of attention," said Rachel with a smile as she turned to go. "And let me know if you want to see a Hartwell noble. The Foxtons have quite a few between us."

"That would be great," Sarah called after her. "Maybe we could meet for a drink."

"Sure," called back Rachel, pushing open the gate. She left the church and made her way to the family farm. She wanted to check on Bailey. He'd started limping again after their last ride. If he wasn't any better today, she would call Ben out to take a look at him.

She opened the kitchen door and for once her mother wasn't in the middle of a mini crisis.

"Hello, love. I wasn't expecting to see you today." Her mother came hurrying over to give her a hug. "Sit down and I'll make you a cup of tea."

"The trip to Newcastle has been cancelled," explained Rachel, bending down to stroke Jenny, who was snoozing in front of the Aga.

"Oh, that's a shame. Actually, I was planning on going on a little trip myself today. Shirley's picking me up, then we're going to collect Joan and drive out to the coast. I haven't been to Scarborough since your dad and I went there for his birthday. Why don't you come with us?"

Rachel smiled. It was the most enthusiastic her mother had sounded in weeks. She was wearing a little make-up too and had put two combs in her hair. As she bustled around making the tea, she almost looked like her old self again.

"No thanks, Mum. I want to check on Bailey's ankle, then I'll either go for a ride or call Ben," she said sitting down at the kitchen table.

"How is Lucy? It must have been a terrible shock for the poor girl, hearing Rob had dug up a skeleton."

"Oh, you know, she's holding up okay," replied Rachel, not really wanting to talk about Lucy or Rupert. "By the way, Mum, do you remember anything about an archaeologist, who was here to study the Druids about thirty years ago? His name was Tarrant."

"Why on earth are you asking about him?" asked her mother, placing two mugs of tea and a plate of flapjacks on the table.

"I was talking to Sarah. She's the archaeologist in charge of the dig where they found the skeleton. She's interested in the Hartwell nobles too. I said I might go for a drink with her."

Her mother looked up, suddenly interested. "Ooh is she nice?"

"Mum, it's not like that—it's just a drink."

"Oh well, it's good to meet new people." She hesitated and gently placed her hand over Rachel's. "I know how fond you are of Lucy, but it would never have worked you know…"

"Mum, please, I know," protested Rachel.

"No, listen, love—even if Lucy was, you know, like you," continued Mary, picking her words carefully, "she's a nice girl, but she isn't the right person for you. You'd spend all your time looking after her, putting her first, and I know that might not sound like a bad thing, but a relationship should be equal. You need someone who can take care of you too."

Rachel listened in silence. Deep down she knew her mother was right, but she simply couldn't bring herself to talk about her feelings right now.

"I told Sarah I'd let her take a look at a Hartwell noble. Where's ours?" she asked, to change the subject more than anything else.

Mary gave her an understanding smile and stood up. "I think it's in the drawer of your father's bedside table. I'll go and have a look." But as she was about to leave the room, there was the sound of a lorry arriving in the farmyard. "Who's this?" she asked.

Rachel got up and went to the window. The lorry belonged to M J Dalton who dealt in fallen stock and took away cattle or horses that were too ill or old to be sold to anyone else. The knacker's yard her father had, called them. It wasn't a company the Foxtons had ever dealt with.

Rachel hurried out into the yard about to tell the men climbing out of the cab that they had the wrong address, then suddenly she saw Max leading Bailey out of his stable.

"What the hell are you doing with my horse?" she shouted, sprinting over.

Max turned around in surprise. "Rachel! I thought you were in Newcastle this weekend."

"So what, you thought you'd get rid of Bailey while I was gone?" she said grabbing the other side of the reins.

"Calm down, Rachel," said Max, in what he thought was his reassuring voice. "He's old and lame, and the stables could be put to much better use. I thought it would be a kindness to do this while you weren't here."

"How dare you!" screamed Rachel, then turning to the two men, who had begun lowering the tail gate of the wagon. "And you two can stop that. Bailey is my horse, and he isn't going anywhere."

The two men looked at Max, who produced a neatly folded sheet of paper from his pocket. He unfolded it and held it up for her to look at.

"Actually Rachel, Bailey legally belongs to your mother, and she agreed with my suggestion."

Rachel's eyes scanned down the page. There at the bottom was her mother's signature.

"What's going on?"

Rachel spun round. Her mother had followed her outside.

"Ah, Mary! You're still here too I see," said Max, trying and failing not to sound disappointed.

"Mum, did you sign this?" Rachel demanded pointing to the sheet.

Her mother peered at it and frowned. "It looks like my signature, but I really don't remember signing anything."

"We discussed it last week. Remember, Mary?" coaxed Max, giving her an encouraging smile. "Remember we talked about what we wanted to do with the stables."

"I do remember you talking about the stables, but..." She trailed off, shaking her head.

"Oh, Mum, how could you be so stupid? They want to have Bailey killed," cried Rachel in despair.

Her mother's hand flew to her mouth and tears welled up in her eyes. "Rachel, I'm so sorry. I just don't remember. I am sorry." Then with a sob she turned and ran back into the house.

"How could you take advantage of her like that?" she hissed at her brother-in-law, then without thinking she reached into the stable and snatched her crop hanging on the wall. She brought it down with a thwack on Max's arm, causing him to yelp in pain and drop the rein. Bailey whinnied and reared up in alarm. The two men moved to grab his reins, but Rachel got there first.

"Come any closer and I'll whack you two as well," she threatened.

"Whoa, calm down!" said one of the men.

"You've gone too far this time, Rachel. You are completely deranged," snapped Max, rubbing the two angry welts that had appeared on his forearm.

At that moment, Jo came jogging past the farm gates with Jack lolloping behind. They both turned their heads at the sound of raised voices.

"Everything all right, Rach?" Jack called out.

"No, they're trying to steal Bailey," Rachel screamed back, close to tears of relief at the sight of her two friends. Jo and Jack ran into the yard.

"What's going on?" asked Jo, while Jack caught his breath.

"We're here to take this horse away, but she won't let us," said the driver, gesturing towards Rachel who still had the crop raised above her head.

"I don't care what it says on that form—Bailey belongs to me," she protested, her voice cracking with emotion. "He made Mum sign it. She didn't know what she was doing."

"I can assure you all the paperwork is in order, Sergeant," said Max, brandishing the forms.

"Max, be a good lad and sod off," said Jack, patting the other man on the shoulder.

"Sergeant?" queried the driver, looking slightly concerned. Jo removed her warrant card from her pocket.

"I'm Detective Sergeant Ormond and as far as I'm concerned possession is nine-tenths of the law." She nodded to Rachel, who was clinging on to Bailey for all she was worth. "So, I'm sorry, gents, but it looks like you've had a wasted journey," she said firmly. The driver and his mate exchanged a look, but neither of them was prepared to argue with the police over an old pony. With a shrug of their shoulders, they climbed back into the cab of the lorry.

"Where are you going?" protested Max as they started up

the engine.

"I'll take this too," said Jo, whipping the form out of Max's hands. "In case it's evidence of coercion."

Max's face flushed red and he pointed to his sister-in-law. "This isn't the end of the matter, Rachel," he said, then turning back to Jo, showed her his arm. "She hit me; you know. That's assault. Those two men are my witnesses. First, she lashes out at her sister and now me. Becky was right about you. You're completely unhinged and frustrated."

Rachel raised her arm again, but Jack quickly stepped in.

"Which bit of sod off didn't you understand, Max?" he asked, pleasantly, as he gently removed the crop from Rachel's hand and wrapped his arm around her shoulder. Max looked like he was about to say something else, but then changed his mind and finally marched away.

"You okay, Rach?" asked Jo.

Rachel nodded, but she still felt close to tears. "Would you two mind hanging around for a while, so I know they aren't coming back? I want to go and check on Mum."

"Sure," said Jack. "I'll settle Bailey back in his stall. Come on, lad, you've had a lucky escape."

Rachel found her mum standing at the kitchen sink, staring out of the window. She went over and put her arm around her.

"I'm sorry I shouted at you, Mum," said Rachel quietly. "I know you didn't sign those papers on purpose."

"Of course I didn't. I know how much you love Bailey." Her voice cracked. "I wouldn't sell him." A tear rolled down her cheek.

"Please promise me you won't sign anything else without

me being here with you," Rachel pleaded.

Mary shrugged off her daughter's arm. "I'm sorry, love, but I'm so tired and my head hurts. I can't talk anymore. I think I'll go and have a little lie-down. Would you mind phoning Shirley and telling her I don't feel up to going out after all?"

Rachel watched her go upstairs. Only a few minutes ago she'd seemed so happy. Bloody, bloody Max! He thought he was so clever. Thinking he'd arranged everything for a time when he expected both Rachel and Mary to be away. She felt sick at the thought of what might have happened to her beloved Bailey if the course hadn't been cancelled too. Rachel trudged back to the stables. Jack was stroking Bailey's nose while Jo was reading through the form she'd taken from Max. She handed it over to Rachel.

"I'd keep hold of this if I was you," she said.

"Thanks," said Rachel quietly, tucking into her pocket.

"Do you want me to stick around?" asked Jack.

"No, thanks. I'll be okay now, but can you tell your mum mine's not feeling up to going out today?"

"No problem. You know where I am if you need me," he said dropping an affectionate kiss on top of her head.

Rachel watched them go, then turned to Bailey, who was contentedly munching a mouthful of hay.

"Come on, you, let's get you somewhere they can't touch you," she whispered. There was no way she'd be able to relax if he stayed here. She'd take him to her cousin Dan's farm up on the moors. Max would never dare try and take him from there. It would mean the stables were now empty, so she'd have to make sure Max and Becky didn't try and bamboozle

Mary into agreeing to their plans, but at least Bailey would be safe.

Bailey's ankle seemed much stronger, but Rachel still didn't want to risk riding him. It would take almost two hours to walk to Dan's, but right now she couldn't think of anything she wanted more than to be out on the moor with her horse and away from everyone else.

DESPITE THE LONG walk and fresh air, that night Rachel couldn't sleep. Dan had been more than happy to take Bailey and she'd left him strolling around the paddock with two grumpy goats. If only everything in her life was as easy to sort out. Rolling over in bed, she listened as the church bells struck twelve, then one, then two. She was so tired, but there was an energy surging through her body that wouldn't let her rest. It wasn't an energy of excitement or anticipation but of fury and resentment, and it wasn't only due to this business with Max and Bailey. It felt like she was angry about everything in her life. Losing her father, worrying about her mother, feeling trapped here in Hartwell. It all felt so unfair. Then there had been the stress over Rupert's disappearance. That nagging doubt that she had somehow missed him that night, the feeling of panic when Dan told her they were digging at the Hayloft. Most frustrating of all though was Lucy herself. They were meant to be best friends. How could she not have seen how she felt about her all this time? Jo and Meera had realised, and they'd only been here a matter of weeks.

Outside it was beginning to grow light and the wood pigeons on her roof were cooing loudly. There was no point trying to sleep now. She climbed out of bed, pulled on her dressing gown and padded down to the kitchen. After switching the kettle on, she made herself a mug of tea and found a quarter of uneaten apple pie in the fridge. She set about eating it with her teaspoon, then started on a packet of chocolate digestives. Now on top of everything else, she'd put on weight. She should really take up running like Jo, who never seemed to get fat despite living on junk food, or eat more healthily like lovely, slim Meera, but she'd probably never be thin.

"Oh for God's sake, stop feeling sorry for yourself," she muttered, standing up and putting the biscuits back in the tin. Maybe she wouldn't ever be thin, but at least she'd had a happy childhood with a loving family, unlike poor Jo—and her problems were nothing compared to Meera's. Holding down a job as a doctor, raising her son alone, whilst all the time covering for her selfish husband. Although, it sounded like he hadn't exactly had it easy either. Like Meera said, imagine having to marry someone you didn't love just to be accepted.

Feeling a little better, she decided to take a shower. That should help her wake up. Then she jumped as her phone gave an unfamiliar ding-dong sound. She picked it up. It was the alert for Facebook Messenger. Hardly anyone messaged her. She squinted at the screen. It was a request from Sarah, the archaeologist. Rachel clicked on the message.

Hi Sarah, here. I was wondering if you'd like to meet up one evening next week. X

Her first instinct was to ignore it. The discovery of the

skeletons had caused enough drama in her life, but then she reasoned that she would probably bump into the archaeologist at some point anyway, and like her mum had said, it was nice to meet new people. She messaged back:

Sure. Sounds good.

In an instant Sarah pinged back.

Dinner at 8 on Friday?

Rachel wrote:

Perfect

She paused, then thought, what the hell, and added an *X*.

CHAPTER THIRTEEN

I T WAS THE day of the event Lucy had organised to show off Hartwell Hall to the wedding organisers and location scouts. The antique longcase clock in the main hall chimed five, which actually meant it was five thirty, but Lucy was already awake. She hadn't been sleeping well since the discovery of the skeleton. It felt like the start of lockdown all over again. Lying awake, listening for a car on the drive or a key in the lock, convinced Rupert would turn up, angry and vengeful. Then as the days passed and the police didn't find him, her dread was replaced with fear that the blow to his head had killed him. She had killed him. He was lying underneath the concrete of the Hayloft's garage. For months she hadn't been able to drive past the village hall without breaking into a cold sweat.

With a shiver, she slipped out of bed. She was still getting used to the bedroom she had decamped to since Tilly had turned her own room into a maternity ward. It had once belonged to Rupert's maiden aunt and was still full of her books and ornaments, but it had a beautiful view of the garden and beyond. She pulled back the heavy velvet curtains. It was already light outside and there wasn't a cloud in the sky, perfect for the visitors wanting to take photos. She watched as a deer strolled across the parkland.

"A hart for Hartwell," she murmured. Surely that was a good omen. She was determined today would be the day she was going to put all thoughts of the past out of her mind and turn around the fortunes of Hartwell Hall. The previous day she had informed Max that she would be handling the event herself. He had arrived with the welcome speech he'd written.

"I thought I'd begin by introducing myself to everyone and I did think I could change my title from estate manager to estate manager and chief event liaison director. With the extra responsibilities, I thought I warranted an extra title." He'd laughed, but Lucy wasn't sure he was joking. She'd surveyed him with a critical eye. He'd been wearing chinos and a blazer, draped over his shoulders as he had a bandage on his arm. His clothes were perfectly normal, but somehow, they didn't look like they belonged to him. It was as if he'd picked up the wrong suitcase at the airport. With a jolt, she'd realised Rob was right—this event was too important to leave to him. She'd switched on one of her brightest smiles.

"You know, Max, you are totally correct. It's unfair of me to expect you to shoulder so much extra responsibility. You've got more than enough to do around the estate already."

"Oh, but that's not what I meant," Max had begun to protest.

Lucy had patted him on his good arm. "No, no I quite understand. Not another word. Leave this event to me. You concentrate on the rest of the estate. While I'm busy here, why don't you go and check those two vacant farms we have on the moors."

She'd seen that he was trying to think of a good reason to stay, but it had eluded him, so finally he'd left with a hopeful: "Call me if you change your mind."

AFTER BREAKFAST, SHE delivered Freddie to Meera, who had offered to look after him. Apparently, he and Krish had great plans to build an assault course for Darwin to play on. When Lucy returned home, she found Joan had commandeered the kitchen to begin preparing the buffet. Jack turned up with some crates of fruit juice and mineral water he'd got from his wholesalers, then Rob and two of his decorators arrived to finish the last-minute jobs to make the house presentable.

Trying not to get under Joan's feet, she made a tray of tea and carried it through to the drawing room where Rob was replacing a rotten windowsill and the decorators were painting over some of the cracks they'd filled the day before. Lucy put down the tray and was about to go and find some room spray or perfume she could squirt round to mask the smell of fresh paint, when Rob called after her.

"Have you got a second?"

"Of course."

"As I drove up this morning, I noticed the glass in one of the upstairs windows is badly cracked. I'll replace it if it's in one of the rooms you are thinking of showing your visitors. It's the one directly above the portico."

"That's the master bedroom and you're absolutely right. It's been broken for as long as I've been here. Are you sure you don't mind replacing it?"

"I wouldn't have offered if I did," he replied easily. Lucy smiled. She was beginning to get used to his blunt way of speaking and had stopped taking offence. In some ways it was like having a conversation with Jo, who had a tendency to be abrupt. Although when chatting to Jo, Lucy never found herself losing her train of thought like she did when she looked at Rob. She showed him upstairs to the bedroom recently vacated by herself and Tilly. Rob placed his tool bag on the floor and looked at her.

"I've been wondering how you are. You know, since they found the skeleton."

Lucy shrugged but couldn't quite bring herself to look him in the eye.

"You really thought he'd been buried there all this time?" he pressed, gently.

"It was so close to the last place he was seen," she replied, quietly. She really didn't want to talk about Rupert today of all days.

Rob frowned. "But the police checked the area when you reported him missing and I've been working on that site almost every day for over a year and a half. I was there all the way through lockdown. Didn't you think I would have noticed if someone had tried to bury a body there?"

She finally looked up at him, her blue eyes wide and haunted as she remembered the feeling of trepidation when Jo drove her down to the Hayloft.

"I know it doesn't make any sense, but when Ben said you'd found a body, I was so sure it was him."

Rob bit his lip. "I'm sorry. I should have come up here

and told you myself when we first saw the bones. I should have known you would think it was him."

Lucy shook her head firmly. "There's no need to apologise. It would have been a shock, however I heard it."

"I suppose." Rob sighed. "It's just that it never crossed my mind that he would still be here. He was always such a selfish sod. I thought he'd headed back to London, to his world of drink and drugs, instead of staying here to look after you and Freddie." He paused. "You believe he's dead though."

Lucy lowered her eyes again. "I honestly don't know what to believe anymore," she whispered.

Rob studied her for a second, then finally turned his attention to the broken pane. "I've got a piece of glass in the truck that I can cut down to fit," he said as he carefully measured the frame.

"Wonderful," said Lucy, relieved by the change of subject. "Anything I can do to help?"

"Go and get the glass," he said tossing his car keys at her. "It's in the back."

"Oh okay," replied Lucy. She hadn't really been expecting him to accept her offer. With keys in hand, she went out to his truck and when she returned with the glass, Rob had already removed the old pane. She carefully laid the glass on the floor next to him and self-consciously perched on the edge of the bed.

"Are you going to watch me?"

"Do you mind?"

"Please yourself. Do you think I might nick the family silver?"

"Ha, ha," laughed Lucy.

As he reached up to put the new glass in place his sleeve fell back to reveal his tattoo. She could see it was a line of Roman numerals. Tilting her head on one side she tried to read them and wished she could remember if X was ten or five.

"It's the date I went to prison and when I got out," said Rob.

Lucy flushed. She hadn't realised he could see her in the reflection of the glass. "Were you in long?" she asked, cringing slightly. Honestly, she sounded like she was at a garden party.

"Three years, but I tried to make the most of my time inside. I studied accountancy and project management, planned the business I wanted to create when I got out. There's nothing quite like having your freedom taken away to make you focus on what you want out of life. When I was released, I got the tattoo to remind me to make every day count."

He turned and raised an eyebrow, giving her a half-smile. "Aren't you going to ask what I was in for?"

"Only if you don't mind talking about it."

"I fractured someone's skull."

"Oh," said Lucy, feeling a prickle of fear run through her. "Did you kill them?"

"No, but he did end up in hospital."

"Were you in a fight?"

She could feel her heart beginning to pound. Rob sighed and Lucy wondered how often he'd told his story.

"Sort of. My little sister's boyfriend had been using her as a punch bag. When I found out, I went round to their house. Before I even knocked on the door, I could hear her screaming inside. I kicked my way in, ran up to the bedroom and pulled him off her. We struggled with each other and he ended up falling down the stairs and cracking his head. I got charged with ABH." He paused. "But the main thing was, Lizzie was okay."

"Is that your sister in New Zealand?"

"Yes. She got in with a bad crowd when we moved to Leeds, but when I was inside, she went travelling and met someone else." He gave a slight smile. "He's a nice guy. A sheep farmer."

"Do you regret it?"

He paused before answering her. "I regret the time I lost, but if someone else I cared about was getting hurt and couldn't defend themselves, I'd probably do the same again. Maybe that makes me stupid."

"No, it doesn't," said Lucy quietly. "I understand that."

She held his gaze for a moment, then slipped off the bed and hurried out of the room, afraid of what else she might say.

AN HOUR LATER, Rob and the decorators had finished. Lucy had managed to avoid being alone with him again. She saw him look at her and frown as she thanked the decorators. Perhaps he thought he'd shocked her, when in fact all she thought was at least he'd paid the price for his crime.

"Good luck," he said as he walked towards his truck. "I'll

call you to see how it went."

She nodded and waved them off from the steps of the portico, then returned to polishing the floor in the long gallery. The dark red walls were lined with the portraits of Rupert's ancestors, staring down at her with accusing eyes.

"It's all right for you—you didn't have to live with him," she muttered, but all she could think about was three years for a fractured skull. What would she do if that happened to her? Who would look after Freddie? Starting to feel sick with worry, she tried to focus on today and not the past.

After the gallery, she moved into the reception hall. A couple of pieces of the black and white chequered flooring were chipped. She was on her hands and knees trying to fix the most obvious one with a black marker pen when a knock at the open front door and a cheery hello told her Guy had arrived.

"Good afternoon, Lucy! I thought I'd call in and see if there's anything I can do to help," he offered.

"Oh, Guy thank you so much," she said getting to her feet. She needed a distraction. "Please could you just take a look around the place and see if there's anything obviously amiss. I could use a fresh pair of eyes. I'll be giving them a tour of the main reception rooms, so the dining room, ballroom, library and drawing room, then upstairs to the long gallery, and the master bedroom."

"You're letting them use your room? Won't that feel a little intrusive?" asked Guy in surprise.

"Oh, it's not my room anymore. After Tilly turned it into her maternity ward, I moved out to the green room in the east wing. Actually, I much prefer it in there."

"Excellent! Well, I shall start my tour of duty and report back, ma'am."

He gave her an exaggerated salute and marched off while Lucy hurried through to the kitchen to help Joan plate up the vol au vents and mini quiches she'd been busy baking.

"These are delicious, Joan," she said helping herself to a still-warm sausage roll. "Just think, if it goes really well today, they might ask us to do the catering too!"

Joan gave a half-smile and raised her eyebrow.

"Us?" she queried.

Lucy grinned back at her. "Don't look like that. I'd help. I could be your sous-chef."

The back door opened, and Bill appeared carrying two wooden trugs full of flowers he'd cut from the garden and greenhouse.

"Do you think this will be enough, Lady H?" he asked putting the trugs down and picking up a quiche.

"They'll be absolutely perfect, thank you, Bill. How's the garden looking?"

"Never better. I rolled the south lawn this morning. It's as flat as a pancake. There'll be no problems for anyone wanting to put a marquee up on it."

As he reached for another quiche, his wife swatted his hand away.

"Stop eating everything, the pair of you," Joan complained in exasperation. "There won't be anything left for when the guests arrive. Now shoo! Out of the kitchen—you're getting under my feet." She wafted her oven gloves at them. Grinning, Lucy and Bill picked up a trug each and they both scuttled out of her way.

Half an hour later, Lucy was in the dining room, arranging the flowers Bill had brought in from the garden in a large vase in the centre of the table when Guy returned from his tour.

"It all looks marvellous, Lucy. Well done! They would be mad not to sign you up," he declared confidently.

Lucy looked up and smiled gratefully. "Do you really think so, Guy? Thanks so much."

"And I'm pleased to see you are taking security seriously too," he continued.

"What do you mean?" she asked as she tried to straighten a drooping gardenia.

"The camera in the main bedroom. I fully understand. You can't be too careful if you are having strangers in the house. If anything though, I thought it was a bit too discreet. It might be better to let anyone dodgy know they are being watched. Prevention being better than the cure and all that."

Lucy shook her head and frowned. "I don't know what you're talking about. There isn't a security camera in the bedroom."

"Yes, there is. I've just seen it."

Puzzled, Lucy headed back upstairs with Guy and sure enough sitting on top of her heavily carved French armoire was a compact little camera. Guy reached up and lifted it down. Its flashing red recording light had been obscured by the wooden trim on top of the wardrobe. He handed it to Lucy.

"I don't understand. Who put it there?" she asked.

"I assumed you'd asked Bill to install it or perhaps some of Rob Harrison's workmen."

"No, they were decorating downstairs mainly. Only Rob was in here fixing the window," Lucy replied turning the device over in her hand. "As for Bill, he's an absolute star when it comes to gardening and general maintenance, but bless him, installing something this technical is beyond him. How long do you think it's been up there?"

Guy fished his reading glasses out of his pocket, took the camera from her and peered at it closely.

"Well, there isn't any dust on it, so not long. I'm afraid I can't see anywhere that says how long it's been recording for. What does this label say? Wi-Fi Motion Sensor."

"So it's transmitting to someone?" asked Lucy, her confusion turning to unease. "I wonder if Jo would be able to find out where to. Or maybe she could check it for fingerprints," she suggested.

"I doubt she'd find any except for yours and mine. Also, I don't think she could investigate unless an actual crime has been committed. I'm not sure how the law would view the fact that it may have been placed there by someone you invited in." Guy hesitated then cleared his throat. "You told me earlier you were no longer using this room as your own, but who else knew?"

"Bill, Joan, and Freddie obviously. Caroline and Rachel maybe. I don't think I mentioned it to anyone else."

Guy removed his glasses and placed a hand on her shoulder. "Look, at the risk of sounding like Caroline, perhaps you should be a little more careful about who you allow to get close to you. You're an attractive, young woman living alone in a large house with her son." He paused, looking and sounding unusually serious. "There may be some, who—

how shall I put this?—would try and take advantage of the situation."

Lucy's hand flew to her mouth as she realised what he was implying. "You mean you think someone thought I still used this room and wanted to spy on me?"

"Now please don't be upset, my dear, but there have been a lot of young men coming and going recently, one or two with rather dubious backgrounds. Now let's focus on what's important. You have a busy day ahead of you. I'll get rid of this camera, and I want you to put this whole business out of your head for now."

Lucy nodded slowly. He was right—she needed to focus on the people due to arrive any minute. They held the key to the estate's success.

"Thanks for being such a good friend, Guy," she said, reaching up and giving him a peck on the cheek.

The MP blushed a little. "My pleasure, Lucy. Now let's go greet your guests. Best foot forward and all that."

The two of them went downstairs and arrived in the reception hall just as the first car was pulling up to the front door.

THE EVENT TURNED out to be a great success. Everyone she invited had turned up. She had been able to answer all their questions and queries. Joan and Bill had done a sterling job of making sure everyone's plates and glasses were full and Guy, bless him, had stayed on to help out. Chatting to various film people about arts funding in the area. They had all been very complimentary about the hall with several promising to be in touch over the next few days. Miraculously, nobody mentioned Rupert's disappearance either. Perhaps they were all too polite or they had forgotten about it, but Lucy had been dreading it coming up in conversation.

She should have been celebrating, but when she curled up in bed that night all she could think about was the camera Guy had found. Who on earth could have put it there? So many people had been in and out of the house, but they were all her friends. Rob was the only person she knew had definitely been in that bedroom. What had Guy said? Someone with a dubious background. Was he thinking of Rob and the time he'd spent in prison?

She jumped as her phone began to ring. It was Rob. He said he would call to see how the day had gone. She stared at the screen for a second, then pressed dismiss.

CHAPTER FOURTEEN

THE OFFICE WAS empty. Everyone else was at lunch. After the first couple of weeks, they'd all given up on asking Jo to join them. She'd spent a frustrating morning investigating a spate of car thefts from holiday cottages on the moors. Grudgingly, she had to admit that on the whole North Yorkshire CID were every bit as committed and professional, if maybe not so intense, as her colleagues back at the Met. However, she'd been teamed up with Detective Constable Darren Dawson. A young pasty-faced officer, who spent more time in the canteen than the office, and always seemed genuinely surprised that a crime may have been committed in his patch.

When he'd presented her with all the evidence they had on the car thefts, Jo had looked at the times, locations, and models and immediately said, "They've been stolen to order, probably for ram raiding."

"Really? How do you know?" Dawson had asked.

Jo had resisted the temptation to snap back, *Because I have a brain!* and instead had said, "All the vehicles are large four by fours and were taken from an area less than an hour away from Leeds. We'd better get on to West Yorkshire and see if we can find a link with anything they're investigating."

Dawson had looked puzzled. "In case they've had lots of vehicles stolen too, you mean?" he'd asked.

"No," she'd explained patiently, "in case they've had a spate of ram raids, which correspond to the times our vehicles were stolen."

Her excuse for staying behind now was that she was waiting for West Yorkshire to call back. She went out into the corridor and looked up and down, to check the coast was clear, before returning to her computer. She wanted to check a couple of things regarding Rupert's case while nobody else was around. Technically, she shouldn't be accessing the file without a valid reason, but what could they do to her next? Send her to Outer Mongolia? Since Lucy and Rachel had told her what really happened the night Rupert disappeared, she'd thought of little else. Then, first thing this morning, she'd received a garbled phone call from Lucy. Something about her and Guy finding a camera in her bedroom, that wasn't really her bedroom anymore, and how Rob and a couple of decorators had been in the house.

"It's just that I know Rob has been in prison and I thought maybe..." Lucy had trailed off, while Jo shook her head at the other end of the line.

"That was for ABH wasn't it? Look, Lucy, I've only spoken to him a couple of times, but Rob really doesn't seem like the peeping Tom type to me."

However, the phone call had got Jo thinking. Could Lucy be the reason for someone wanting rid of Rupert? Either to protect her or because they simply wanted her husband out of the way, so they could make a move? She tapped away at the keyboard of her computer and accessed the original file notes for Lord Rupert Hanley's missing persons investigation.

The notes weren't easy to follow. The officers involved kept changing. She could remember what it was like back then. Colleagues went home every day, told to self-isolate with even the mildest of symptoms. It had been incredibly frustrating.

Some of the witness statements were confusing too. Quite a few couldn't be sure of the time they'd seen Rupert. It was to be expected. People had a lot on their minds. They were focused on their own problems and how they would cope. She read the statement Lucy had given. There was no other information to contradict it and it tallied with statements from the members of the parish council. As far as the investigating team were concerned Lucy was simply an anxious young wife, worried about her missing husband.

Jo found the part where they had searched the area surrounding the village hall. Sniffer dogs, trained in locating bodies, had been sent in and particular attention had been paid to the foundations that had been dug on the land Rob owned, but nothing had been found.

Interestingly, considering Lucy's phone call, the only 'person of interest' they had interviewed was Rob Harrison. Jo wasn't entirely surprised. He had form, Rupert was last seen close to his property and the two men had business dealings. His alibi was that he'd been drinking in the White Hart. Jo thought for a moment. Jack had said it was busy that evening. Rob might have been able to slip out unnoticed. What if he'd found Rupert and finished him off before Rachel arrived? Maybe Lucy wasn't being completely paranoid after all.

She continued scrolling through the notes. She wanted to see which officer in London they had liaised with. Her eyes scanned down until she saw a name she knew well. DS Simon Spencer. They'd had a brief fling a couple of years ago and still hooked up occasionally. He was an arrogant sod, but he might be one of the few guys at the Met still willing to take her call. She picked up her phone and dialled his number. After what seemed like forever, he finally answered.

"All right, darling. How you doing? Is it grim up north? You got yourself a whippet yet?" Jo raised her eyes to the ceiling. Simon had always mistakenly believed he was hilarious.

"Did you investigate the disappearance of Lord Hanley?"

"Still not a fan of small talk, I see, Jo. Yep, your lot asked me to look into what happened to Lord Snooty and find out if he was down here."

Jo's jaw tightened. Your lot. It hurt to be reminded she wasn't part of the Met anymore.

"To be honest, I'd have disappeared too if I was him," continued Simon.

"Why's that?" she asked.

"He owed money all over the city and to some people you really don't want to be in debt to."

"Dealers?"

"Yep, including your friend Roy Sutcliffe. It sounded like his lordship had quite the habit."

"But you didn't find any sign of him returning to London after he was reported missing?"

"Nope. He usually stayed at his club, one of those fancy

places in St James, but that was closed during lockdown. We found a couple of his suppliers, but they hadn't heard from him."

Begrudgingly, Jo thanked him, then clicked off her phone, only for the one on her desk to ring immediately. It was her opposite number in Leeds confirming that there had indeed been a spate of ram raids on jewellery shops in the north of the city. All the cars used were found burnt out, but they matched the models she had given them. Jo promised to send them all the details she had. At least she was making progress somewhere, but from what she had learnt today, it was far from certain that Rupert was dead. If he'd just done a runner, then there was no point reporting what Lucy and Rachel had told her. He could well turn up and then she'd have got them into trouble and made herself look a prize idiot all over again.

THE NEXT MORNING, Jo decided to extend her run by going through the churchyard. As usual, Jack was puffing along behind her, his new puppy strapped to his front in a weird sort of papoose.

"You do know that isn't the conventional way to walk a dog, don't you?" she said as they took a breather. Jo sipped her water, while Jack flopped down on the wooden bench nestled amongst the graves.

"Ben said not to take him out for a few days following his last jab," he panted, "besides he's only got little legs, but I thought it would do him good to get used to our route."

"Have you thought of a name for him?"

"No, I thought I'd let you do the honours."

"If you insist." She glanced around. The nearest grave was marked by a simple headstone with the name Joseph Baxter Tarrant. "How about Baxter?"

Jack nodded his head slowly as he considered her suggestion. "Yeh, Baxter. I like it." He lifted the puppy out of the papoose and kissed him on the nose. "What do you think? Baxter? Baxter? Who's a good boy, Baxter?" The little puppy pricked up his ears, put his head on one side and began wagging his tail furiously. "I think he likes it too," announced Jack with a grin. Jo shook her head as she continued to study the gravestone.

"Maybe it's not such a good idea. This guy died before he was forty. Who was he anyway?"

"No idea," replied Jack, glancing at the dates on the stone. "I was only little when he died. It's not a local name either. Another Hartwell mystery for you to solve. Speaking of which, have you found out anything about your noble?"

"No," said Jo. "Honestly, I haven't given it much thought. The way I see it is, I've made it this far without knowing who my parents are—what's the point in trying to find them now? I needed them when I was a kid, but not anymore, so whether there's a connection to Hartwell or not makes no difference. I've got no intention of staying here." She paused and looked across at him. "You do know that don't you, Jack?" she said gently. She had grown quite fond of him, and she really didn't want to hurt him.

"I know," said Jack lowering his head and stroking Baxter's ears. "You've always made that very clear." Then he looked up and smiled. "But you're here now. And if Scotland Yard ever wake up and realise that they were mad to let you go, Baxter and I can always follow you down to London."

"Then I really will have you arrested for stalking," she joked. For a second, she considered mentioning Lucy finding a camera, but then remembered he was good friends with Rob.

"I thought you were great the other day, by the way. How you saved Bailey. That was amazing," he said and looked at her with such admiration she felt herself flush in embarrassment.

"Thanks, but I hoped my career would involve more than saving horses from the knacker's yard."

"I know, but it must feel good to help people—you know, make a difference."

Jo shrugged. She'd never really analysed how she felt about her work other than it always felt good to catch the bad guys.

"Anyway," continued Jack, "I've been thinking, while you are still here, you should definitely visit the Druid caves on the moors. Remember I told you we all used to play there as kids? They used to be open all the time, but a couple of hikers injured themselves climbing up there, so now the national park only lets people go up in the summer holidays when they have enough volunteers to show people the safest route. We could make it Baxter's first proper walk. What do you think?"

"Maybe, let's see," said Jo, wishing he would stop trying to get her to commit to things.

"We could take a picnic," continued Jack.

Jo raised her eyebrows. "I'm really not a picnic kind of a person."

Now it was Jack's turn to raise his eyebrows. "Rubbish! You always order a ploughman's for lunch. It's basically the same, except you'll be sitting on a rug instead of in the beer garden."

Jo took a last sip of water and stretched her legs. "All right, all right, if I'm still here when they open these caves, I'll go, but you've really built them up to be something special. I'd better not be disappointed."

And with that she sprinted off.

CHAPTER FIFTEEN

IT WAS STILL warm and sunny when Meera left the surgery. The air was full of the scent of freshly cut grass from the cricket pitch across the road. At least she couldn't complain about her commute home. A two-minute stroll to her cottage compared to being stuck in Bradford's rush hour traffic for at least an hour. She collected Krish from the after-school club on the way and heard all about the wormery he was making, while silently praying he didn't ask to bring it home. Ben was coming for supper later, but first Krish needed to Skype his father.

Meera had received a phone call from him a few days ago. She didn't know how he'd got her new number, but she suspected it had something to do with her brother. It was Dev's father's birthday and his whole family would be celebrating at the Kumars' palatial house in Amritsar. As soon as travel restrictions had been lifted, instead of visiting Krish, who he hadn't seen since Christmas, Dev had flown straight to India.

"Dad will be expecting to see Krish on his birthday, so I'll Skype you," he said. "Please make sure he's presentable and on time—you know what my father's like."

Meera sighed. She knew exactly what Surendra Kumar

was like. He was a loud bully, who used his wealth to control and intimidate his three sons.

"I've told my family that you have been sent to the countryside to continue your important vaccination work."

Meera rolled her eyes. Was there no end to the lies he could come up with? At the other end of the line, Dev continued to whine.

"I have to say, trying to explain why you are no longer living in the house my father bought for you has been very stressful."

Stressful, thought Meera. Stressful is taking your little boy to A&E with an asthma attack so bad he can barely breathe, after a full day of treating patients yourself. How many times had she had to do that alone while he was partying with men half his age in the nightclubs of Manchester?

DEV'S HANDSOME FACE smiled out from the screen of the laptop. It was night-time in Amritsar and there was clearly a party going on. There was loud music playing and lots of figures moving about in the background.

Meera had told herself that it was important Krish kept in contact with his paternal family, but hovered out of sight in the doorway, refusing to get drawn into any more of Dev's lies herself.

"Do your twelve times table for Dada, Krish. And why aren't you wearing your Manchester United shirt?"

Meera shook her head. Why did Dev have to treat his son like he was a performing monkey? If he'd been around more often, he would have known that Krish had been able to do all his times tables since he was six. As for the football shirt, that had been his Christmas present to Krish. It was two sizes too small and Krish didn't even like football.

Dev carried the laptop outside to show Krish a series of flash cars owned by his father and brothers. Krish smiled and nodded, his skinny little frame hunched over the computer as a succession of relatives he barely knew pointed to their BMWs and Mercedes. He had no interest in cars and got confused by what he was supposed to call his uncles. Out of politeness he called everyone auntie and uncle, but proper relatives had special names, so he should call Dev's older brother Thaya and his younger brother Chacha, but Krish often got them mixed up, resulting in laughter from his uncles and a frown from his father.

With a pang, she wondered if she should have tried harder to teach Krish about his heritage. Growing up, she'd felt like she was walking a tightrope between the two cultures of her old home and her new one. She was always the quiet, bookish one amongst her loud, outgoing Indian relatives, but never feeling she entirely fitted in with the English people she met either. Even though she had been fluent in the language when she arrived here, she still found the humour, or the habit of understating one thing and overstating another, confusing. She remembered one of the surgeons at the first hospital she'd worked in describing being stuck in a traffic jam for ten minutes as 'an absolute bloody nightmare' but losing his wife of forty years to a younger man was merely 'a bit of a blow'.

Meera had dressed in western-style clothes since she was

a teenager. However, her mother, despite moving to this country over twenty years ago, still insisted on wearing a sari, even in the depths of a Yorkshire winter, when it was hidden under several chunky-knit cardigans. As Krish was the first member of the family to be born in the UK, Meera had hoped things would be easier for him.

Dev suddenly disappeared and Aishwarya, his mother, took his place on the screen. With her kohl-rimmed eyes and wearing a peacock-blue silk sari, she looked every bit as beautiful as the Bollywood actress who shared her name.

"Look at you, Krishnan, so handsome like your father!"

Aishwarya was extremely superstitious and believed boys' names should have even numbers of letters, so it was always Krishnan and Devinder. Over the years, Meera had thought about her mother-in-law a lot. Dev was her favourite son— she must have known who he truly was. Had she chosen Meera for him because she was known to be so obedient, so dutiful, such a good girl. Had she been picked to be Dev's route to a better life in the UK away from the threat of prosecution? Meera wondered if she would have done the same for Krish.

Finally, the call was over and to Meera's relief there had been no mention of her son going over to India.

Krish closed the laptop. "Did I do okay, Mum?" he asked, looking anxious.

"Of course, I'm very proud of you, as is your dad and his family. All of them," she reassured him with a smile and a hug. "You didn't introduce them to Darwin," she added as the ferret jumped from the sofa on to Krish's shoulder.

"No," said Krish, stroking his pet's ear as he went upstairs, "I didn't want Dad to laugh at him. He probably wouldn't think he was a very good pet."

A surge of anger rose through Meera. With Dev it was always about how things looked to other people, how it reflected on him. That was the real problem. Not that Dev was gay, but that he was selfish. When he'd explained how impossible it was to live in a country where it was illegal to be who you really were, she had sympathised and believed him when he'd said they would be the best of friends and raise Krish together. But he'd lied. He'd used her, and now he was using their son.

From upstairs Krish shouted down. "If Ben's coming for tea, can we have lasagne?"

"Of course," replied Meera with a smile. It seemed she was more upset by the video call than her son.

As THE END credits of *Sense and Sensibility* began to roll, Meera wiped a tear away with the back of her hand and sniffed. A yawning Krish had gone to bed an hour ago, and it was just the two of them. Ben passed her the box of tissues on the coffee table and shifted in his seat to look at her.

"Are you okay?" he asked.

Meera sniffed and nodded. "It doesn't matter if it's a happy or a sad ending. I always cry," she replied.

Ben smiled and adjusted his glasses. "I've been meaning to ask you something. I heard the Leeds Playhouse are putting on a production of *Wuthering Heights* next month at the Brontë Parsonage in Haworth. I was wondering if you would like to go?"

Meera dabbed at her face as she shook her head. There was nothing she would enjoy more than watching a performance of one of her favourite books in the home of Emily Brontë, but Haworth was only twenty minutes away from Bradford. She couldn't risk being seen by some who knew her, or Dev.

"Thank you, it's a lovely idea, but I don't think I should," she said. "I'm not sure it would be appropriate."

Ben's face fell.

"I see, well at least I know now," he said.

"Know what?"

"That you don't want to go out with me. I suspected that was the case, but I thought if I invited you to something I knew you'd really like and you said no, then I could be sure. What's the phrase you used about the bat? You put me out of my misery."

"I'm sorry, if I..." she stammered, but Ben shook his head.

"It's not your fault. I like you a lot and—" he gestured around the room "—there are no pictures of your husband anywhere, and you and Krish barely mention him, but I read too much into the situation. You were never misleading though. Mainly you treat me like I'm Krish's friend."

"Do I?"

"Yes, I don't mind. I know I can be a bit accident-prone—" he gave her a lopsided smile "—but earlier, you told me to blow in my lasagne because it was hot."

Meera raised her hand to her face in horror. "I'm sorry. I honestly don't realise I'm doing it." She paused. She was going to have to tell him. He deserved an explanation. "You see, I'm not used to having a man around. I'm used to it just being me and Krish."

"I understand. It must have been a big change, for the two of you moving here without your husband."

Meera shook her head. "No, I mean before we moved here too." She hesitated and felt the heat rise to her cheeks. "Krish was conceived on our wedding night, but after that Dev and I didn't live together as man and wife. We didn't have a physical relationship."

Ben stared at her for a moment. "May I ask why? Was there a medical reason?"

"No. Dev is gay, but obviously I didn't know that when I married him."

"Then why stay married to him?" asked Ben, his face creased in confusion.

Meera sighed, wishing it was that straightforward. "It's quite complex," she said. "There's a lot to take in."

Ben gave her an encouraging smile. "I don't like to brag, but I'm quite good at following complex stories. I got through *War and Peace* without losing track of any of the characters."

Meera smiled at him, trying to lighten the mood. She took a deep breath and then let the whole story come tumbling out. She told him about how she didn't want to hurt her family, and how Dev was terrified of his family's reaction and being disinherited and finally about his veiled threats to take Krish away. When she'd finally finished, she looked at him, but she couldn't read his expression.

Then at that moment, his phone bleeped. He glanced at

the screen. "I'm sorry, but I have to go. I'm on call," he said reaching for his coat and heading for the door. He paused and looked back. "Thank you for explaining. You're right— there is a lot to take in." And with that he left.

Meera stared after him, then sank back into the sofa as she heard the door close with a firm click. She didn't blame him for leaving. He was probably relieved to be called out. It was clear he'd decided she had far too much baggage. Why would he want to take on someone with so little experience of men and whose gay husband refused to divorce her? No wonder he'd gone as quickly as he could. She curled up, resting her face against the cushion and quietly began to sob at the unfairness of it all. After a few seconds, she felt some- thing cold and wet touch her hand. Darwin had come to see why she was making strange noises. Krish must have forgot- ten to lock his cage again. Meera scooped him and hugged him to her chest.

"It looks like it's just the three of us from now on," she whispered as another tear slid down her face.

CHAPTER SIXTEEN

LUCY TURNED UP the radio, spinning around in front of her bedroom mirror as she sang along to Kylie Minogue. Scattered across her bed were the results of this morning's shopping trip to Harrogate. Two new dresses, a pair of strappy gold heels and a bottle of her favourite perfume. That morning's post had delivered a contract from one of the film and television location companies and two provisional bookings for weddings in August.

She'd bumped into Guy after she'd dropped off Freddie at Meera's for a sleepover that morning. When he'd heard about her news, he'd offered to take her out to dinner to celebrate, so she'd decided to go to Harrogate and treat herself. On the way home, she'd spotted Rachel walking through the village and had pulled over to tell her friend all her news, but Rachel had seemed a bit indifferent.

"Do you want to come and have a G&T and see what I've bought? You can help me choose what to wear tonight."

Rachel had shaken her head. "No, I'm going to have a drink with Jack." And with that she'd disappeared into the pub. She hadn't told Lucy to have a nice time or even made a snarky comment about Guy.

Standing in front of the mirror Lucy picked up the blue

dress and held it against her, then the purple. Lucy could barely remember the last time she'd had the chance to dress up in something new. Yes, definitely the blue. She glanced at the clock by her bed. There was just enough time for a nice long soak in the bath.

GUY HAD BOOKED them a table at one of York's Michelin-starred restaurants down by the river. He was waiting for her at a table in the bar.

"You look lovely, Lucy," he said kissing her on the cheek and handing her a gin and tonic.

"Thank you. It's new," admitted Lucy.

"Well, it's a beautiful colour on you, but I liked the purple too. Now will you excuse, me a second. The constituency chairman is over there. I must go and say hello."

Lucy smiled and watched him cross the restaurant floor, shaking hands and stopping to chat at various tables. She took a sip of her drink. It felt good to be out properly again, eating at a place that didn't serve chips with everything and where everyone else had dressed up too. She glanced down to admire her new strappy heels. You could just see the little tattoo of a deer on her ankle. She'd had it done in Amsterdam a few years ago, when she was more than a little bit drunk. Joan and Bill had looked after Freddie, so she and Rachel could have a girls' weekend away. She'd hoped Rupert would think it made her sexy and exciting again. He'd accused her more than once of being boring and mumsy since she'd had Freddie. However, when he'd seen it, he'd only sneered and told her it made her look like a footballer's wife.

She gave her head a shake. She didn't want to think about Rupert tonight. Instead, she thought about Rachel. She'd been very quiet and moody recently. Maybe they could have a night out to cheer her up. It would be a good excuse to wear her new purple dress too. She reached for the menu, then froze. How did Guy know about the purple dress? Nobody had seen it, not even Freddie or Joan. She'd bought it after she'd spoken to him that morning.

Then she heard Freddie's voice in her head. *"Mummy, I think there's a man outside."*

Her heart began to race. She glanced around the room. Guy was talking to someone in the far corner. He had his back to her. Quickly, she stood up and hurried to the door.

"Is anything wrong, madam?" asked the young man on the reception desk.

"Migraine," said Lucy, raising her hand to her temple, but not looking back. She dashed out the door and through the gates of Museum Garden. Yanking her new shoes off, she sprinted along the winding path in her bare feet, ignoring the people who pointed and stared until she reached Marygate, where she'd parked her car.

She climbed in and with shaking hands turned on the ignition. Thank God she'd refused Guy's offer and driven herself here tonight. With her foot on the accelerator, her mind raced along with the car. Images flashed through her head. Freddie telling her he'd seen someone outside. Guy showing her the camera he'd found. There must be a camera in her room. That's the only way he could possibly have known about the other dress.

The sun had disappeared from the sky and it was growing dark when she arrived back in Hartwell. She slowed down as she passed the pub. Through the window she could see Rachel at the bar. Rachel would know what to do. She bumped up on to the pavement and hurried inside. The place was heaving. Rob, Dan, and Jo were standing together chatting to Jack. Rachel was sitting a little apart from them, a large glass of wine in front of her. Lucy pushed her way towards her.

"Rach! Thank God you're here. I need your help."

Rachel looked up and blinked several times, but seemed to be having trouble focusing. "Aren't you meant to be on date with Guy?" she replied.

"Yes, that's what I want to talk to you about. Something's happened. I need your help," whispered Lucy urgently.

Rachel began slowly shaking her head and she still wasn't smiling. "No not again. I'm not helping you again," she said, her words slurring into each other.

"Are you pissed? Have you been in here since I saw you earlier?"

"What do you care?" said Rachel, her voice rising. Jack and the others looked over. Unsteadily, Rachel slipped off the bar stool, knocking over her wine glass and pointed a finger at Lucy. "You don't care about me. You just want a man to look after you and you always go for the same pompous, arrogant creeps. You are a terrible judge of character."

"Getting a bit loud, Rach. I think you've probably had

enough," said Jack quietly, leaning across the bar. "Maybe you two should have this conversation outside."

"Yes," agreed Lucy. "Let's go outside, Rachel."

But Rachel shook her head firmly. "No, I don't want to talk to you anymore. I'm done with you. I won't waste any more of my time. I'm going to find someone who'll love me back."

And with that she staggered past the other gawping customers and out the back door. Lucy stood in stunned silence, staring after her.

"I'll go and make sure she's okay," said Jo jumping from her bar stool and following Rachel outside.

"I don't understand," Lucy stammered, turning in bewilderment to Jack, who couldn't quite meet her eye as he mopped up the spilt wine on the bar. Lucy suddenly became aware that everyone else in the pub was staring at her. She felt the heat rise to her cheeks. She couldn't handle this right now. Without a word, she ran out of the front door. She heard Rob call out her name, but she didn't stop. All she wanted to do was get home.

She needed to find out what was going on with Guy. Had she gone completely mad, or had he been stalking her all this time? She didn't know which was worse. She jumped back into her car, a million thoughts swirling in her head. What the hell did Rachel mean, find someone else to love? She was her best friend. Oh God, she couldn't think about this right now. She needed to get home.

Heavy raindrops splashed her face and there was a distant rumble of thunder as she ran to unlock her back door. The place was in darkness. Tilly and Pickle came running to greet her as she pushed open the door. She raced upstairs to her bedroom and shuddered at the sight of the discarded purple dress. Her eyes scanned the room. Where the hell could it be? She checked on top of the wardrobe, behind the curtains, nothing.

Then in the dressing table mirror she saw the reflection of the bookcase that covered the far wall. It was crammed full of hundreds of books, lovingly collected by Rupert's aunt. *"I can't remember the last time I picked up a book."* The words she'd said to Guy at the quiz immediately came back to her. She turned around and walked towards the bookcase, her eyes skimming the shelves. She froze. There it was. The little black lens peeping out at her. She lifted the copy of *Emma* that was resting on top of it and picked up the camera. It was the same as the one that had been placed on top of the wardrobe in the master bedroom. It had been wedged on top of *Middlemarch*, the lip of the hardback cover obscuring the light. She felt sick. It had been pointing right at her bed. He'd been watching her sleep, seen her in her underwear.

There was a loud clap of thunder and a flash of lightning. Rain was now pelting against the windowpane. Lucy grabbed her phone out of her pocket. She was about to dial 999, but hesitated. The police would want proof it was Guy. Was the camera enough? She couldn't risk not being taken seriously. Jo would know what to do. She cursed herself for not staying in the pub to talk to her. Quickly she scrolled through her list of contacts and clicked on her friend's name.

"You know I'm very disappointed in you, Lucy."

She spun around. Guy was standing in the doorway. He was holding a shotgun.

"Hang up, Lucy," he said sternly.

"Guy please put the gun down," she said in a loud, clear voice, praying that if Jo picked up, she would hear. Then very slowly she lowered the hand holding her phone and slipped it back into the pocket of her jacket. Guy stood there staring at her.

"Why did you have to go running off like that? You made me look very silly. We could have enjoyed such a lovely evening together. For a moment, I thought you might really be ill, but no, you went running back to the Hart."

He began walking towards her very slowly.

"You've been watching me," stammered Lucy, her mind racing, trying to understand how he knew she'd been to the pub. Guy put his head on one side and smiled.

"Of course I have, Lucy. Somebody had to look after you. You're such a flighty little thing. I had to think of a way to keep track of you."

He reached out and stroked her cheek. Lucy took a step back, remembering all those times she'd just happened to bump into him.

"My phone," she stammered. "The night at the parish council. I didn't lose it. You took it." Her heart was racing. She could barely breathe.

"I borrowed it for the evening. It was for your own good. Such a clever app and I knew you'd never realise."

"And the other camera? You let me think one of my friends put it there."

"I really couldn't have you associating with a builder, Lucy. That's what I mean. Left to your own devices you keep making silly mistakes. Is that why you went to the Hart? To see Harrison?"

He looked angry now. There was a dangerous glint in his eye. She knew that look. She needed to keep him calm. She attempted a smile and tried to keep her voice normal.

"Of course not. I went to speak to Rachel. Jack called me to say she'd had too much to drink. I was worried about her. I'm sorry, I should have explained, instead of leaving you. Why don't we go down to the library? I'll pour you a drink and explain everything."

Guy narrowed his eyes, but then he nodded. "You've always been a good friend to the Foxton girl. You have a good heart. Yes, a drink would be nice."

Lucy breathed a sigh of relief. All those years of appeasing Rupert hadn't been wasted. Keeping him calm, so he wouldn't shout and swear and wake up Freddie. Oh, thank God her little boy was safe with Meera tonight.

They made their way down the elegant staircase. Lucy had wondered if she dare make a run for it, but he was walking behind her and he still had his gun. She jumped at another flash of lightning and a loud clap of thunder, then the muffled sound of her dogs barking. Guy must have shut them in the kitchen. At the bottom of the stairs, she slowly crossed the hallway to the library, Guy's heavy footsteps echoing behind her on the marble floor. She flicked the light on. Her mouth was dry. She needed to find a way to get him to put the gun down. If she gave him a drink, he might relax, and he'd only be able to hold it with one hand.

"Whisky? Or G&T?" she asked, her voice artificially bright.

"Whisky," replied Guy. "Then I think we should talk

about our future."

Lucy nodded, her hand shaking as she lifted the decanter and splashed the amber liquid into the glass. She turned to hand it to him. Guy smiled then they both froze as they heard heavy footsteps in the hallway.

"Lucy, are you okay? The back door was open and your dogs were going crazy in the kitchen."

It was Rob. Lucy felt a wave of relief sweep over her.

"I knew it," hissed Guy, his face now full of fury, "I knew you were involved with that yob. He's a criminal for God's sake."

Her relief turned to panic as Guy stepped behind the door and raised his gun.

"Rob, don't come in!" she yelled, but it was too late. Rob was walking through the door towards her, dripping wet, his hair plastered to his face.

"You looked upset when you left the pub," he began, then seeing her stricken face: "What's wrong?"

"How dare you come up here uninvited," snarled Guy, appearing from behind the door.

Rob spun around. "What the hell! Guy, put the bloody gun down!" he said raising his hands and positioning himself between Lucy and the gun. Guy continued to slowly advance, the gun pointing at Rob's chest.

"Please, Guy," pleaded Lucy.

"I haven't waited patiently all these months, for you to come muscling your way in."

There was another flash of lightning outside, then the sound of splintering glass as Jack came crashing through the French doors followed by Jo.

"Stay back," shouted Guy, swinging the gun towards them. Lucy took her chance and hurled the whisky at his face. He gasped and raised his hand to wipe his face. As he did, Rob lunged and grabbed at the gun, as Jo and Jack got to their feet.

"It's over, Guy," yelled Jo.

Guy suddenly leapt onto the sofa, then jumped off the back and fled out through the broken French door. Jack, Jo, and Rob all chased after him. Lucy slowly sunk down on to the sofa, put her head in her hands, and tried to steady her breathing. In the distance, the faint wail of sirens was getting closer and somewhere a door slammed. A few minutes later, there was the sound of running feet on the terrace. Lucy looked up. Jo and Rob reappeared in the doorway, both dripping wet.

"It's okay, we got him," Jo said breathlessly and looking surprisingly cheerful. "Jack tackled him to the ground, and Rob held him still while I cuffed him. Uniform have arrived to take him away."

"Where's Jack?" asked Lucy.

"He bashed his dodgy knee and by the sound of things he probably cracked a couple of Guy's ribs when he landed on him. Joan and Bill heard all the commotion and came up. She's in the kitchen now, strapping up his knee."

Rob had poured out a brandy for each of them and handed one to Lucy.

"This is getting to be a habit," he said with a smile.

"Thank God you phoned me," said Jo, clearly on an adrenaline high. "I could hear you loud and clear. We drove up here as quickly as we could."

"He had a camera hidden in my room and he's done something to my phone so he can track me," Lucy said handing her phone to Jo.

"I might have to hold on to this and get forensics to take a look," she said, "and I'll go and check out the camera too, but first I'd better take this brandy to Jack," she continued, heading out the door, then as an afterthought: "To think you suspected Rob of spying on you, when all the time it was that old creep."

Embarrassed, Lucy turned to look at Rob, but his smile had disappeared.

"It was the day you fixed the window in the bedroom," she stammered, trying to explain. "After you'd left, Guy told me he'd found a camera in there."

Rob took a step towards her. "You really thought I'd hide a camera to spy on you? Like some sick peeping Tom?" He raised his hands in exasperation. Lucy flinched. Rob stared at her for a second. "And that I could hit you? You know, Rachel was right. You are a terrible judge of character." He turned on his heel and strode out as Joan came hurrying in.

"Oh you poor thing!" she cried. "Jo and Jack told me all about it. Are you all right, love?"

Lucy curled up on the sofa, hugging her knees to her chest. Tears began streaming down her face and she couldn't stop shaking.

Joan sat down next to her and took her hand. "It'll be all right, love. It's all over now."

"It was such a horrible shock and now everyone is so angry with me," she sobbed.

"Now that's not true."

"Rachel and Rob hate me. They think I'm stupid and they're right. Rachel never liked Guy. I should have listened to her."

"Now stop that. Rob doesn't hate you; he's just had his pride dented. As for Rachel, well that was bound to end in tears at some point. You were never going to love her the way she wanted you to."

Lucy stopped crying and stared at Joan in surprise. "You knew how she felt about me?"

"I think everyone did, love."

"Everyone except me. Poor Rachel." Lucy began crying again.

"There, there," said Joan. "Everything will be all right, you'll see. You know what they say, not all storms come to disrupt your life, some come to clear your path. It will all look better in the morning."

CHAPTER SEVENTEEN

R ACHEL WOKE UP with a thumping head, a churning stomach, and a mouth that felt like sandpaper. It took her a few minutes to realise that the banging she could hear wasn't just inside her head. Staggering downstairs in her pyjamas, she opened the door to find Jo standing there holding a flask and a plate covered in tin foil. She pulled a face as soon as she saw Rachel.

"Bloody hell! Do you feel as bad as you look?"

"Worse!" groaned Rachel, shielding her eyes from the bright sunlight. "Come in."

Rachel went through into the kitchen and flopped down on a chair. Jo followed her through and placed the flask and plate on the table.

"Shirley sent me over with this. She would have come to check on you herself, but she's fussing over Jack. Strong black coffee and a bacon sandwich. Best cure for a hangover."

Rachel closed her eyes, feeling sick at the thought of trying to swallow anything. Images of the night before flashed through her mind. Jack leaning across the bar, Nora's face full of glee and Lucy's stunned expression. She groaned.

"What about public humiliation and heartbreak? Have

you got anything for that?" she asked looking up at Jo.

"All coming back to you, is it?" she said not unsympathetically.

Rachel was going to nod her head, then thought better of it. "Unfortunately, yes. I can't remember getting home though."

"You ran out into the beer garden. I followed you, but you'd already legged it over the wall. After a minute, I saw your bedroom light go on, so I guessed you were okay."

Rachel leaned back in the chair and groaned again. That explained the nasty graze on her ankle that was beginning to throb.

"I'll never be able to show my face again."

Jo unscrewed the top of the flask and sloshed some coffee into the plastic cup. "Maybe it's a good thing. You know, finally get it all out in the open. Are you going to eat that before it gets cold?" she asked gesturing to the bacon sandwich.

Rachel shook her head and winced as a police car, its siren blaring, sped past her window. She took a grateful sip of the strong coffee. "Hang on. Why did you say Shirley is fussing over Jack? Is he ill?"

"Not exactly, but he's bashed up his dodgy knee."

"How?"

"That's what I'm here to tell you. I arrested Guy last night. Turns out he's been stalking Lucy for ages," said Jo, taking a huge bite out of the still-warm sandwich.

Rachel stared at her blankly for a second.

"What are you talking about? He took her out for dinner last night."

"Then he'd followed her home. It seems he'd got it into his head she was seeing Rob. He'd set up a camera in her room, been tracking her phone. He had a shotgun and everything. He'd gone full psycho."

"Oh my God! Is she okay? Is Freddie?"

"Yep they are both fine. Freddie was at Meera's all night."

At that moment, Jo's phone bleeped. She looked down at the screen. "It's work. I'll have to go. Look, take a shower and some paracetamol, then go see Lucy."

"She won't want to see me."

"Yes, she will."

With that Jo shoved the last of the sandwich into her mouth and headed out the door. After she'd gone, Rachel drank some more of the coffee and tried to process everything Jo had just told her. She'd never liked Guy, but she hadn't had him down as being totally unhinged. She felt a pang of guilt. Lucy had come to her for help last night and all Rachel had done was blame her for her own unhappiness. Taking Jo's advice, she knocked back two tablets with the last of the coffee and headed upstairs to the bathroom.

As she left her cottage, she slipped on a pair of sunglasses and began walking towards Hartwell Hall, hoping the fresh air would help clear her head. She passed the shop where Nora was outside sweeping the path.

"Well, you certainly made a spectacle of yourself last night," she called out.

"Yeh, and didn't you just love it," retorted Rachel, not bothering to stop.

"And then her ladyship up at the Hall went and got our

MP arrested. Poor Mr Lovell."

"I think you'll find he did that all by himself," Rachel yelled back over her shoulder. Only Nora could take the side of a stalker.

SHE FOUND LUCY sitting in the shade of the old horse chestnut tree where Rob had built the platform and rope swing. She was leaning against the tree trunk with her eyes closed. Her face was almost white, except for the violet-tinged circles beneath her eyes, and there was a bandage on her hand.

"Are you okay?" Rachel asked, gently.

Lucy opened her eyes and smiled. "Hey, you. I'm fine. What about you?"

Rachel flopped down next to her. "I've got the mother of all hangovers, I'm racked with guilt and embarrassment, but apart from that, yeh, I'm fine too. What happened to your hand?"

"I cut it last night, clearing up the broken glass," explained Lucy, pointing across the garden to the terrace, where Freddie was helping Bill board up the broken French window, "Jo and Jack made quite an entrance."

Rachel gave a little shudder. "Thank God they did. And that Freddie was with Meera. Does he know what happened?"

"All I told him was that Guy had done something bad and the police had arrested him."

"What did he say?"

Lucy smiled. "That he didn't like him much anyway and that Rob and Ben are nicer and Jack's much funnier. It seems my little boy is a far better judge of character than I am, thank goodness."

Rachel felt herself flush in embarrassment, as her words from last night came back to her.

"I'm so sorry, Lucy. I shouldn't have said what I did last night, and I should have been here for you when you needed me. I never liked Guy, but I didn't think he was completely barking. What a creep!"

Lucy began flapping her hands. "Please, Rachel, I don't want to talk or even think about him. And it's me who should be sorry. I've been a terrible friend. Totally selfish. I've been so wrapped up in my own problems. I wish you'd told me before."

"I couldn't. I knew you didn't feel the same, but I couldn't bear to hear you say it. To have you shatter the illusion and that's all it was really, an illusion. I'm beginning to realise that now. For a long time, everything in my life was crap. Charlotte leaving me, Dad getting injured, not being able to finish uni and go travelling, then the whole Covid mess and losing Dad. You were the only good thing, so I focused on you and well, I guess you are easy to fall in love with."

"I really am sorry, Rachel. I know how it feels to love someone and not have them feel the same."

"Rupert?"

Lucy nodded sadly. "I know at the end I hated him, but for years I hoped he would fall back in love with me and things could be like they were when we were first married."

She hesitated and glanced across at Rachel. "Are we okay? We are still friends, aren't we? I couldn't have handled what happened and got through these last few months without you."

Rachel nodded. "We're good, but we maybe shouldn't see each other quite so much for a while." Lucy opened her mouth to protest, but Rachel held up her hand. "I need to clear my head. Term ends soon and if Mum's okay, I'm thinking of going away somewhere. God knows I could do with a change of scene."

Before Lucy could reply, they were distracted by a shout and a figure in a tank top and combats hurrying towards them.

"Oh God! It's bad news, isn't it?" asked Lucy as soon as Jo was in hearing distance, "You've had to release Guy, haven't you?"

"No," replied Jo slightly breathlessly, "but we haven't been able to question him either. He's in hospital. They need to operate on his ribs, and he's torn a ligament in his ankle too, but I'm not here about Guy." She hesitated. "They've found Rupert."

Lucy and Rachel both stood up. Rachel began to feel queasy again.

"Where?" she asked.

"In that old Druid cave. The volunteers were opening it for the summer, when they found him."

"Is he dead?" asked Lucy.

"Yes," Jo replied. She looked down at her feet. "He's been there a while, so they'll need to use his dental records to be sure."

"Oh God!" Lucy leaned back against the trunk of the old tree and put her head in her hands.

"They did find this though. It matches the description you gave when he disappeared." Jo unfurled her hand to show a gold signet ring in a clear plastic evidence bag. It was engraved with oak tree and hart, the Hanley family's crest. Lucy took one look at it and silently nodded her head.

"How did he end up in the cave?" asked Rachel, silently cursing herself. Of all the days when she needed to be able to think straight and her brain was foggy from the hangover.

"You tell me," replied Jo, slipping the evidence bag back in her pocket. Rachel and Lucy both stared at her.

"You think we took him up there?" asked Lucy incredulously.

Jo shrugged. "Maybe when Rachel went to look for him, she found his body and decided to hide it."

"But she could never have managed on her own and I couldn't have helped. I was here with Freddie. Joan was here too, but she had to go back to the gatehouse. I would never have left Freddie on his own," stammered Lucy, her voice rising in panic.

Jo held up her hand to silence her. "We don't know yet if he died in there or somewhere else and was moved there afterwards." She hesitated. "Look, I shouldn't be telling you this, but I've spoken to the pathologist who's at the scene. She found a hairline fracture to his skull."

"Oh no, oh no," whispered Lucy as she slumped to the ground. Jo knelt down next to her and spoke softly.

"Look, they don't know if that's what killed him yet, but if there is anything else you haven't told me. I need to know."

"I've told you everything," protested Lucy, close to tears.

"What about the spade you hit him with?" asked Jo. "Could it have had his blood on it? I checked the notes. There was no mention of it when they searched the site."

Lucy's face wrinkled in confusion, but behind them Rachel cleared her throat. She was going to have to come clean. Jo twisted round to look at her.

"I took it," she said. "I saw it when I was looking for Rupert. You're right. It had blood on it, and I assumed Lucy's fingerprints, so I took it and threw it down the old well."

"You never told me," gasped Lucy.

"You had enough to worry about," Rachel explained with a small shrug.

"And why didn't you mention it before?" demanded Jo.

"Honestly, because I wasn't sure we could trust you," said Rachel. "We all know how much you need to do something impressive to get back to London. I thought if you went straight back to your superiors and repeated what we'd told you, it would still be your word against ours.

"So why tell me now?"

Rachel took a deep breath. "I suppose now I'm hoping if we need you, you'll help us," she replied.

Jo held her gaze for a moment then nodded. "The coroner will be holding an inquest. I'll let you know, as soon as I hear anything."

Then she turned and walked back across the garden. Lucy and Rachel watched her go.

"Maybe I should go straight to the station and confess everything now," said Lucy quietly.

"Don't you dare," snapped Rachel, who was in desperate

need of more headache tablets. "You were only protecting yourself. And besides, neither of us had anything to do with him ending up in that cave."

RACHEL CLOSED THE playground gate behind her and waved goodbye to her colleagues. It was the last day of term. The others were all going over to the White Hart to celebrate. Normally, she would have joined them, but since the discovery of Rupert's body, the village had been buzzing with gossip. Everyone seemed to have their own theory as to what happened. The press had been sniffing around and Rachel had never seen Nora so happy. Lucy had barely left Hartwell Hall. She'd kept Freddie at home for the last few days of term too, after a nasty comment from Jared Parkin about the Hanley curse striking again.

Rachel started walking back to her cottage. She thought of visiting her mum, then noticed Caroline heading through the farm gate. She hadn't seen the older woman since they'd found her son's body and Rachel had no idea what she should say to her. The previous evening, Rachel had frightened herself to death googling what the sentence was for aiding and abetting a criminal or assisting an offender. She gave a shudder and prayed it wouldn't come to that.

When she arrived home, she flopped down on to her bed and exhaled. To complicate things further, today was also the day she'd arranged to have dinner with Sarah. She'd received a message a couple of days ago with the time and name of a little French restaurant on Castlegate in York. Since then,

Rachel kept picking up the phone to cancel and then putting it back down again. Should she really be going on a date with everything else that was happening? She looked up at the map on the wall with its paltry number of pins and suddenly thought, *Sod it! My life's been on hold long enough.* If she was going to lose her freedom, she may as well enjoy herself while she could.

She went to the bathroom and ran herself a deep bath. Then she brushed her teeth and shaved her legs. It was years since she'd been on a date and nerves started to flutter in her stomach. With her wet hair wrapped in a towel she squeezed herself into her hold-you-in pants, cursing the apple pie she'd eaten and all that wine she'd downed. She opened her wardrobe and tried on, then discarded, almost every piece of clothing she owned. In desperation she called Meera for some advice. Meera arrived as she'd finished drying her hair and immediately picked out a plain navy linen dress and then dashed home and returned with a pale pink silk scarf that complimented Rachel's arms, tanned golden brown from riding. They had teamed the outfit with a pair of navy kitten heels that Rachel hardly ever wore.

"You should wear your hair loose," instructed Meera. "It's your best feature. You'll look seductive."

Rachel snorted, but did as she was told and undid the clasp holding back her hair. "I'd settle for thinner," said Rachel, grimacing in the mirror as she shook out her hair and smoothed the dress down over her hips.

"Nonsense," tutted Meera, "it's good to be curvaceous. Sarah must think so or she wouldn't have asked you out in the first place."

"I don't suppose you want to come in the taxi with me, do you? I could do with someone to boost my confidence."

Meera gave her a smile. "I'd love to, but I should go. I've left Jo looking after Krish. When I popped back, they were listening to rap music and feeding Darwin popcorn. I don't think she's done much babysitting before."

"Oh, I assumed Ben was with him."

"No," said Meera shaking her head, "I decided to tell him the truth about my situation, when he came for supper a couple of days ago, and well, I haven't seen him since."

"Oh, Meera, I'm sorry," said Rachel.

Meera gave a little shrug of her shoulders. "It's fine. At least I know where I stand. Now don't worry about me. Have a wonderful time. You look lovely," she said, kissing Rachel on the cheek before she went.

Rachel stood outside on her doorstep waiting for her taxi. Ben pulled up on the other side of the road and made his way over. He raised his hand in greeting. "Evening, Rachel. You look different."

"It's the hair."

"Ah yes. Well, it's nice."

Rachel rolled her eyes. "Skip the compliments you silver-tongued charmer. What are you playing at?"

"What do you mean?"

"Meera! She poured her heart out to you and you just walked out on her."

"I didn't just walk out," he protested, adjusting his glasses. "I said there was a lot of information to process. It seemed a good idea to take some time, think things through, before coming up with a plan."

"She isn't some cat with a tricky skin condition. You should go and talk to her."

"I will," he replied earnestly, "I promise, but I need to check something with Rob first."

Then he turned and walked straight into the White Hart. Rachel watched him go and shook her head. *Men!*

THE TAXI DROPPED her off on Clifford Street. It was only a short walk to the restaurant, but she was already regretting the heels. They added two inches to her height, but she was struggling to negotiate the city's cobbled streets in them. Finally, she arrived at the restaurant. She checked her reflection in the glass door, took a deep breath and stepped inside. A waiter showed her to the table where Sarah was already waiting for her. She stood up and kissed Rachel on the cheek.

"Sorry I'm late," Rachel apologised immediately. "Race day traffic."

"No, it's fine," replied Sarah, with a wave of her hand. "I hope this place is okay. I wasn't sure what food you liked, but I thought you can't go wrong with French, and I've checked the menu—they do have vegetarian options if you don't eat meat."

As she chattered away, Rachel realised with relief that Sarah was just as nervous as she was.

She smiled. "No, I'm a true farmer's daughter. I don't think my father would ever have forgiven me if I told him I was a veggie."

Sarah laughed and looked down at her menu. Rachel

took a moment to study her properly across the table. Her curly hair was the same colour as an Irish setter. She'd piled it loosely on top of her head, but a few strands had escaped and there was a smattering of freckles across her nose. She was wearing an olive-green shirt-style dress and like Rachel, her arms were tanned from being outside. The waiter appeared and took their order and returned a moment later with two glasses of wine.

"What shall we drink to?" asked Rachel.

"How about Hartwell?" suggested Sarah. "I thought it was a sleepy little place when I first arrived, but there seems to have been one drama after another."

"Okay," agreed Rachel raising her glass. "To Hartwell."

"How's your friend?" asked Sarah. "I heard it was her husband they found in the cave."

"She's doing okay," replied Rachel briskly, not wanting to talk about Lucy or Rupert tonight. "What happened with the photo of the archaeologist's grave you posted? Did anyone respond?"

Sarah shook her head; another curl came loose.

"No, unfortunately, but it was a long shot."

"I asked my mum if she remembered him, but we got distracted by another drama, before she could tell me."

Sarah raised an eyebrow. "Really? What sort of drama?"

Rachel found herself telling the story of Max trying to take Bailey, then about how upset Mary had been and how worried she was about her mother's health. Sarah listened intently, reacting first with shock and then with sympathy.

Over the moules marinieres and saumon provençale they continued to chat about their families and work. Sarah was clever and funny, but she was a good listener too. Rachel told her how she longed to see more of the world.

"Are you planning on going anywhere over the summer holiday?" asked Sarah.

"I'd love to get away, but I want to make sure Mum's okay before I book anywhere."

Sarah put her head on one side. "In a couple of weeks, I'm going out to Peru. It's kind of a busman's holiday. I'll be working on a dig out there, but also have the chance to do some sightseeing. A friend of mine is running the dig. She's always looking for volunteers to help out. They provide food and accommodation. You only need to pay for the flight out there. Why not come too."

"But I'm not an archaeologist," said Rachel.

Sarah shrugged. "It doesn't matter. You could help out photographing artefacts or with admin stuff. I'm no expert in Incan civilisation, but I'm desperate to see Machu Picchu."

"It does sound wonderful." Rachel sighed. The ancient, abandoned city was at the top of her list of places she longed to see, but could she really contemplate a trip to South America, with everything that was happening at home?

They finished the meal with tarte au citron and coffee, then Sarah walked Rachel to the taxi rank.

"Thank you for a lovely evening," said Rachel feeling shy all of a sudden.

"It was my pleasure," replied Sarah, "and think about what I said about the trip to South America. It would be great if you could come too." She leaned forward and softly brushed her lips against Rachel's cheek. Sitting in the back seat of the taxi, travelling through the city and out into the country, Rachel let herself imagine a future that took her to exciting places with a lovely red-haired archaeologist. All the things she'd dreamed of suddenly didn't seem so out of reach. If everything went well with the inquest and her mum, then she might finally be able to escape Hartwell.

THE NEXT MORNING, Rachel was up early. She pulled on her jodhpurs and T-shirt, feeling happier than she had in a long time. She was going to drive up to Dan's to take Bailey for a quick hack, but first she wanted to check on her mum. She'd missed a call from her last night. There had been no mishaps for a couple of weeks, and happily for Rachel, Max and Becky had both been keeping a low profile since the Bailey incident. If Mary still seemed okay, then Rachel had decided she wouldn't wait for the outcome of the inquest, she would tell Sarah she wanted to go to Peru too.

Rachel pushed open the farmhouse door.

"Hi, Mum. It's only me," she called cheerfully, then froze. Her mother, still wearing her dressing gown and slippers was sitting at the kitchen table with her head in her hands sobbing quietly.

"Mum, what is it? What's wrong?" asked Rachel.

Mary raised her head and looked at her daughter. "Rachel, I'm so worried. I've been awake all night. I don't know what's wrong with me. I keep forgetting things and losing things and making stupid mistakes." She gulped between sobs. "I thought I was getting better, but before going to bed last night, I went to the freezer in the utility to take some lamb out. I thought I'd let it defrost overnight and make a shepherd's pie today, but when I got there everything was ruined. The freezer had been unplugged. I called you and your sister. Becky thought I'd mentioned clearing it out, but I can't for the life of me remember doing it."

Rachel hurried over and wrapped her arms around her mother. She hated to see her so frightened like this, but at least she had admitted there was a problem. Rachel had been worried about saying anything for fear of upsetting her, now finally she could do something.

"Shh, Mum, don't cry. It'll be all right. We'll take you to see the doctor and get you some help."

"What if it's, you know... What if they say it's something they can't fix?"

Frightening words like Alzheimer's and dementia hung in the air between them.

"Whatever they say, we'll cope, Mum," Rachel reassured her. In truth, Rachel had no idea what she would do. All she did know was her mother needed her and she was staying right here. Sarah, and any thoughts of going abroad with her, would have to be pushed to one side. She phoned Sarah later that evening to tell her so.

"I'm really sorry about your mum, Rachel, and that you won't be coming to Peru." She paused. "Would it be okay if I emailed you while I was away?"

"Of course. I'd love to hear about everything you're doing out there."

"Maybe if there's good news about your mum, you might still make it over for a week or two."

"Maybe," replied Rachel, trying to sound positive, but good news seemed to be in very short supply at the moment.

CHAPTER EIGHTEEN

M IRACULOUSLY, MEERA'S AFTERNOON appointments had finished early. The morning rain clouds had cleared and the sun was beginning to break through the clouds. She stepped neatly over a puddle in the middle of the path. She had half an hour before she picked Krish up from the holiday club they were running at the school. There was enough time for a cup of tea and to change out of her work clothes and into something more casual. Perhaps the two of them could drive into Helmsley and get an ice cream. Her heart sank a little as she remembered Ben taking them there on the day Krish found the bat. She hadn't seen or spoken to him since he'd left so abruptly that night. It had only been a couple of days, but with all the drama about Guy and then Rupert's body being found it felt much longer.

As she turned on to her lane she froze. Nish's car was parked outside her cottage. Her brother was leaning against it fiddling with his phone.

"What are you doing here?" she asked.

"Mum made me drive them over," he replied, not bothering to look up.

"Where are they?"

"Through there," he said nodding towards the little

wooden gate that led to her back garden.

Her parents were sitting in silence on the wooden bench beneath the apple tree. Her mother was in her favourite green sari, her father with his neatly clipped moustache and swept-back hair looked greyer and older than she remembered.

"Mum, Dad, is everything all right?" she asked.

Her mother stood up. "No, it is not. This silly business has gone on long enough. I don't know what is going on with you and Dev, but we haven't seen you for months."

"I'm sorry, Mum," Meera began to apologise.

"A wife should be with her husband," interrupted her father, sounding belligerent. His wife turned to him and threw her arms up in despair.

"She can't very well help it if her husband has gone back to India. Do you want her to disappear over there too and take our only grandson with her?" she demanded in a tone Meera had never heard her use towards her father before. "We would never see them. It would be like being locked down again. Meera has always been a good girl—she deserves our support."

Meera didn't say anything. Her eyes remained fixed on her father. Slowly he rose to his feet and opened his arms. "Your mother is right. You've always been a good girl. Dev should not have abandoned you."

Meera flung herself at him and burst into tears. "Oh, Papa, I've missed you," she sobbed, as her father stroked her hair.

"I'm sorry too," he said softly. "I should have chosen someone better for you. Not someone who is never here to take care of you. You worked so hard helping people all those months—he should have been with you and Krish, not in Manchester. He promised me he would make things right between you, but instead he disappeared to India."

At that moment, Meera longed to tell her father everything, but then Nish began to snigger, earning himself a swift clip around the ear from his mother and reminding Meera it might be better to remain silent.

"Good well, now that is sorted out, you can take us to see our grandson, Meera," said her mother decisively. Wiping her eyes, Meera led them along the cobbled path up to the school and watched as Krish came running out, surprised and delighted to see his grandparents. He was even excited to see Nish, who for some reason he thought was cool.

When they arrived back home, Meera made tea while Nish was despatched with a shopping list to the nearest garden centre, after her mother had declared that the cottage garden contained nothing useful. He returned with pots of mint, coriander, basil, sage, parsley, and thyme. Meera watched from the kitchen window as her mother instructed her brother where and how to plant each one. Krish had introduced Darwin to her father, who much to everyone's surprise was quite taken with the ferret. The two of them were attempting, not very successfully, to teach him to sit and roll over. Meera couldn't remember when she'd felt so content.

HER PARENTS DIDN'T leave, until after Krish had gone to bed. Meera waved them goodbye with a promise to see them again soon. She turned the key in the lock and was about to begin her nightly routine of checking lights and switches were off, when there was a knock at the door. Thinking her parents must have forgotten something, she opened it immediately and found herself staring at a huge bunch of white roses.

"Hello," said a soft Scottish voice from behind the flowers, "I know red are more romantic, but they only had white."

Meera took the bouquet to reveal Ben, looking a little sheepish.

"What are you doing here?" she asked.

"I came to apologise for, well, for not coming sooner," he said looking down at his feet. "That's what the flowers are for. They've wilted a bit. I was going to come earlier, but saw you had company. I wasn't sure if you would want me to meet your family."

"They are beautiful, thank you," she said. "Would you like to come in?"

She took the flowers into the kitchen, and he followed her through, carefully ducking his head under each beam.

"I've been thinking about everything you told me, and I've come up with a plan." He handed her a picture of a beautiful castle with a mountain behind and lake in front. "What do you think?"

"It's lovely, but why are you showing it to me?" she asked.

"I've booked it for us. For a holiday."

Meera stared at him dumbfounded.

"I got the idea from Colonel Marsden," Ben continued.

Meera's hand flew to her mouth. "You didn't tell him about me and Dev, did you?"

Ben frowned and shook his head. "No of course not. Why would I? But he'd called me in because one of his older Labs wasn't very keen on the new puppy he got from Lucy. He kept growling when it went too close to his bed, that sort of thing. I thought the older dog was simply being territorial, so I suggested he take them to neutral ground, to get to know each other. The colonel took them for a long walk across the moors and it worked a treat. They are absolutely fine now. And that got me thinking. Maybe that's what we need. Somewhere away from the village, where neither of us can be on call, where you aren't worried about seeing someone you know, somewhere we can relax. Neutral ground."

Meera looked at the picture again. It was like something out of a fairy story. Forget Lizzy Bennet or Catherine Earnshaw—staying here, she would feel like Cinderella or Sleeping Beauty. A smile slowly spread across her face.

"It's a castle. You've actually booked us a castle?" she asked incredulously.

"It's not really a castle. It's a large farmhouse, but it's built in the Scottish baronial style."

"It has turrets!"

"It does," agreed Ben, with a grin. "I thought you'd like that. And there's a loch and a mountain and there are red squirrels in the woods behind. I know how much Krish wants to see them in the wild. I grew up not far from there—

I thought I could take him fishing. We might even get to see a golden eagle. It belongs to a couple of friends of mine. They rent it out for holidays, but they'd had a cancellation."

"But what about Dev and the divorce and everything? If he finds out I've taken Krish away on holiday with you, he might try and use it against me."

"Personally, I think he's making empty threats to scare you, but if it's okay with you, I asked Rob to get one of his guys to check all your window and door locks are as secure as possible while we are in Scotland. That way Krish won't think there's anything to worry about. You don't mind me asking him, do you?"

Meera shook her head. "No, it was very thoughtful of you, but well you've gone to an awful lot of trouble. What if you and I, you know, it doesn't work out? If we don't get on?"

"I think that's very unlikely. I get on with everyone from Caroline Hanley to Frank the milkman, and I happen to think you are lovely, even if you do worry far too much," he said. Meera was about to interrupt him, but he raised his finger. "However, if we're only ever destined to be friends, we'll still have had a nice holiday and Krish will have seen red squirrels."

"But what if..." Meera began again. Ben gently placed his finger on her lips.

"Let's take one step at a time."

CHAPTER NINETEEN

THE CHURCH CLOCK was striking midnight. Jo sat on the bench in the graveyard drumming her fingers against the wooden seat. She couldn't decide what to do and it was driving her mad. At least out here she could smoke and think without anyone disturbing her. She lit another cigarette, inhaled deeply and leaned back. The inky black cloudless sky was sprinkled with stars. She'd never really noticed them when she lived in London. There was a rustle in the bushes and a little brown rabbit hopped out. He surveyed Jo for a few seconds, his nose twitching, then hopped over to a nearby grave to munch on the floral arrangement that had been left there.

Jo took another drag on her cigarette. She wished she could work out how Rupert got into that cave. Jack had been right; it was beautiful up there. Beautiful, but not easy to access. There was a padlocked gate at the bottom of the steep winding path that led up to it, and the entrance wasn't easy to find either. There was no way Rachel and Lucy could have carried a dead body up there in the middle of the night and no way Lucy would have left her little boy on his own either.

Despite what Rachel and Meera might think of her, she wasn't so ambitious that she wanted Lucy to go to prison for something she didn't do. The coroner had asked the pathologist for a full report, but Jo's gut feeling was that a whack from a spade wasn't what killed Rupert. However, Lucy was such a bag of nerves, it was quite possible she'd confess before the coroner gave his verdict. Even if she used self-defence as justification, she could still be sent to prison. Poor Freddie would be left without either parent. Jo knew what that felt like. She'd never had much to do with children before, but Freddie was a nice kid. The best way she could help him and his mother was to find out how Rupert ended up in that cave.

She kept replaying different scenarios in her head. Perhaps after his confrontation with Lucy, Rupert had gone to the place where he'd played as a child and overdosed either accidentally or on purpose while he was there. Forensics had said there were traces of white powder on his clothing. Then she'd wondered if his dealers that Simon had spoken to when the investigation switched to London could be involved. Was there a chance that he'd panicked about being stuck in Yorkshire with no coke, arranged to meet them in the cave, and they'd got violent about the money he owed?

She shook her head. No, if dealers had killed him, she was sure there would be more obvious signs of violence to the skeleton. They'd found him lying on his back with his hands by his sides. It was a peaceful pose, and it made her wonder if it was possible he'd been taken there after he'd died.

However, her favourite theory involved Guy. What if his obsession with Lucy had driven him to kill her husband? He'd been in the village that night, supposedly at home on a conference call with his advisors. However, she still hadn't been able to question him about his alibi or anything else. Her theory was just a hunch and she'd need solid evidence before taking it to her superiors, but it felt like her best hope of solving the case and putting Lucy in the clear.

Rachel's words about not knowing if they could trust her had felt like a slap in the face. Nobody had ever questioned her integrity before, but then outside of the police, nobody had ever asked her for help before either. She dropped the butt of her cigarette on to the path and ground it under her foot. Then she stood up with a loud groan, startling the rabbit, who scurried away. This was the problem with having friends. They made your life very complicated.

INCONCLUSIVE, INCONCLUSIVE, INCONCLUSIVE! Didn't they know any other words? Jo was flicking through the post-mortem report on Rupert's remains. The hairline fracture to his skull: inconclusive. Evidence of drug use prior to his death: inconclusive. Even though the white powder found on his clothing was definitely cocaine. Evidence that he had died in the cave: inconclusive. In her pocket, her phone began to ring. It was Lucy.

"The coroner has sent me a copy of the post-mortem report. What does it mean?" she asked her voice full of panic.

"That they don't know how he died," explained Jo.

"But why don't they?" persisted Lucy.

Jo sighed. She was going to have to spell it out for her. "There wasn't any soft tissue or internal organs to test. All that was left was his skeleton and clothes." There was silence at the other end of the line. Jo lowered her voice. "It's good news, Lucy. Did you do as I told you and stick to the statement you made when he went missing?"

"Yes," said Lucy, so quietly Jo could hardly hear her. The coroner had asked for statements from Lucy and the members of the parish council, who as far as anybody else was concerned, were the last people to see Rupert. Dr. Robertson had also been contacted at his villa in Portugal. He confirmed that he was the Hanley family doctor, but that he hadn't seen Rupert professionally for years. He'd made no mention of Lucy's injuries. Fortunately for them, unlike Meera, he'd never associated her cuts and bruises with domestic violence. There was no reason for the coroner to think Lucy might want her husband out of the way.

"Look," said Jo, trying to sound less harsh, "this time tomorrow it should all be over. The coroner will have delivered his verdict and unless its unlawful killing, the police won't investigate. Okay?"

"Okay," repeated Lucy.

"Take care. I'll see you tomorrow."

She slipped her phone back into her pocket and went to get a coffee from the machine out in the corridor. It took her money, but only gurgled loudly before spitting boiling water into her cup.

"Stupid bloody thing!" She slapped her hand against it in frustration. It was looking more and more likely that the investigation into Rupert's death would be closed. This might be good news for Lucy, but it wouldn't help Jo's career. It felt like everything was going against her today.

This morning, she'd heard that the magistrates had turned down her request for the warrant to search Guy's house. She had been on such a professional high when she arrested Guy. A sitting MP was an impressive collar, especially as a firearm was involved. The story had made the nationals and she'd even had a call from Simon congratulating her.

However, since then, Guy's expensive legal team had quickly sprung into action. They had found a psychiatrist, who recommended he be detained under the Mental Health Act, so he was still in a hospital rather than a cell. She hadn't been able to interview him about the stalking charges, let alone find out exactly what he was doing the night Rupert disappeared. Even if they managed to charge him, it was looking increasingly likely that he'd be declared unfit to stand trial.

The full weight of his party had swung behind him too. She was convinced there was political pressure behind the magistrate's decision. The press had changed their tune as well. They were beginning to portray him as a confused, overworked public servant instead of a psychotic stalker. The way things were going, she couldn't see how she would ever get back to London.

THE DAY OF the inquest began badly for her and got progressively worse. Despite much shouting and wheel-kicking, her car had refused to start that morning. She'd managed to cadge a lift to Northallerton with Dan Foxton. However, if she'd known he was going to sing off-key along to Capital

FM all the way, she would have called a taxi. To make matters worse, his spaniel on the back seat had rested his head on her shoulder all the way, leaving her covered in saliva and dog hair. Now she was stuck in a stuffy office, two hours into a talk about sheep rustling. The droning voice of the officer leading the investigation was almost sending her to sleep. Finally, he declared they could break for lunch. Jo headed straight out of the station and across the marketplace to the town hall where the coroner's court was being held.

The place was packed. Most of Hartwell had turned up. Jo watched them all from her position at the back of the room. Lucy was sitting on the front row, dressed in black, her pretty face pale and drawn. Rachel was on one side of her looking calm, but serious. Behind them was Caroline, also in black and her expression impossible to read. Nora Parkin was there on the front row too, tucking into a packet of liquorice allsorts. Jo also spotted several members of the local and national press.

The coroner entered the court and opened the inquest. He was a tall, thin man with wisps of hair clinging on to his bald head. His voice was almost as monotonous as the officer's she'd left behind. He began by stating where and when Rupert's remains were found and then went over each statement and piece of evidence. Jo watched the hands of the clock on the wall slowly tick round. He'd been talking for nearly twenty minutes.

"I now come to my conclusion," he said.

Lucy turned around and shot Jo an anxious look. Jo attempted to give her a reassuring smile.

"In the case of Lord Rupert Hanley, I declare an open

verdict."

Lucy's shoulders slumped in relief and Rachel exhaled loudly, while Caroline remained rigid and impassive. Jo watched as the three of them filed out amid the hum and chatter of the other attendees.

"So, we still don't know how he ended up in that cave?" asked Becky.

"Let us not forget that the Lord does move in mysterious ways," replied Reverend Davenport.

"What does an open verdict even mean?" grumbled Nora, clearly disappointed at the lack of drama.

"That the damn fool coroner couldn't make his mind up," muttered the colonel.

Jo sighed. What it meant was that unless any other evidence was uncovered, the police would no longer be investigating the death of Lord Rupert Hanley. Lucy and Rachel were safe and she was still stuck in Hartwell. She was the last to leave the courtroom. As she stepped outside into the late afternoon sun, she saw a familiar figure waiting for her. Jack was leaning against his sports car and raised his hand as she walked towards him.

"I thought you might need a lift home."

"How did you know my car was out of action?" she asked.

"Always so suspicious," Jack said shaking his head. "The whole village heard you swearing when you tried to start it this morning."

"Oh well, okay then a lift back would be good," agreed Jo.

"Excellent! On the way we could drop into this great little wine bar I know in Harrogate."

"Harrogate isn't on the way," she said, then shot him a quick smile, "but hell, why not? It doesn't look like I'm going anywhere else anytime soon."

"I knew you'd give in eventually," said Jack, beaming as he held the door open for her, and Jo slid into the smooth leather passenger seat. As she'd told herself a million times, he wasn't her type, but after the day she'd had, she deserved some fun.

CHAPTER TWENTY

Lucy stretched out her legs as she leaned back in her chair on the terrace. She had changed into jeans and a T-shirt as soon as she returned from the coroner's court. She couldn't quite believe it was over. All those months and months of worry swept away with a few words spoken by a balding man in a town hall. She should be feeling relieved, but she just felt numb. Numb and tired.

Meera sat next to her, quietly sipping her tea. Freddie and Krish were sitting under the horse chestnut tree munching their way through a plate of Joan's shortbread. Rachel had travelled back with her from Northallerton, but had wanted to go and check on Mary as soon as they got back to the village. Lucy had invited Caroline to join them for tea too, but her mother-in-law had briskly replied, "No thank you, Lucinda, I shall be meeting with Reverend Davenport. Now the body has been released, plans need to be made for the funeral.

"Oh, perhaps I could help you?" Lucy had suggested, although in truth she'd been so wound up about today's verdict, she'd completely forgotten the need for a proper burial.

"That won't be necessary, Lucinda, thank you. You have

absolutely no experience of organising a funeral. Your time would be far better spent caring for Freddie. He's all that matters now."

"Where's Jo?" asked, Lucy turning to Meera. "Shall I give her a call? It feels like she should be here too. I know you and Rachel both doubted her at first, but I don't think I'd have got through this whole thing without her. She's been amazing at explaining everything to me."

"I heard she's finally given in and let Jack take her out," replied Meera with a smile. "Dan said he saw them driving off together towards Harrogate."

"It's about time," said Lucy. "I think they make a lovely couple."

They sat in silence for a few moments.

"How's Freddie coping? Does he understand about today?" asked Meera tentatively, nodding towards the rope swing where the two boys were playing.

"Sort of. I tried to keep it simple. I told him a man was going to try and work out what happened to Daddy. He still hasn't cried though. I don't know if that's a good or bad thing." Lucy sighed.

Meera placed her cup down and took a couple of business cards out of her pocket. She handed them to Lucy. "You might find these people useful. If either of you need to talk to someone," she suggested gently.

Lucy looked at the cards. One was for a grief counsellor who specialised in talking to bereaved children; the other was for survivors of domestic abuse. Lucy felt tears welling up in her eyes.

"Thank you," she said, quietly, "I wish you had been

here back then."

"So do I," said Meera, reaching out and giving her hand a squeeze.

They watched their sons playing for a while, before Lucy turned to Meera.

"What are you and Krish up to over the summer? Any holiday plans?"

A shy smile spread across Meera's face. "Actually, we do, but are you sure it's appropriate for me to talk about it, given what's happened today? I can save it for another time," asked Meera, who looked like she was bursting to say something.

"I think it's the perfect time. I've had enough of coroners and inquests and post-mortems. I only want to hear happy things for the rest of the day. Come on, spill," demanded Lucy.

"Well, if you are sure," said Meera, sitting up a little straighter in her chair. "Ben is taking Krish and me away for a couple of weeks. To the Scottish Highlands. Ben is going to show Krish where red squirrels live."

Lucy looked at her in surprise.

"You're going on holiday with Ben? Wow, no wonder you can't stop smiling."

"Would you like to see the place he's booked? It has turrets."

She carefully removed the picture she had been carrying around in her handbag.

"Wow," repeated Lucy, "it looks amazing!"

"It does, doesn't it," agreed Meera.

"Who knew Ben could be so romantic," said Lucy, then raising an eyebrow as she studied the picture. "It looks like it has a lot of bedrooms. Have sleeping arrangements been discussed? Could the ten-year drought be over?"

"Really, Lucy, you are as bad as Jo," tutted Meera, but was still not able to stop smiling. "We're taking things slowly. One step at a time." She paused. "And if it's not meant to be, then we'll remain friends and I'll be very lucky. Since moving to Hartwell, I've made more friends than I've had in my entire life."

Lucy raised her cup of tea. "To friends!"

"Friends!" Meera echoed.

MEERA AND KRISH left when the sun began to set and Joan and Bill also came to say goodbye to Lucy, after checking she was okay for about the tenth time that day.

"You'll feel better soon," Joan had said as she'd hugged her. "Time is the greatest healer."

"That's just it," said Lucy with a heavy sigh, "it feels like I've been in mourning for years. I was grieving for the man I married a long time before Rupert disappeared. Maybe that's why I don't feel particularly different today. My marriage died a long time ago."

Joan nodded and looked down at her hands. "You had some very difficult times, love. I wish we could have done something sooner."

Lucy looked puzzled and shook her head. "You couldn't have done anything. I hid what was happening, partly because I was ashamed and partly to protect Freddie from the truth. You weren't to know what Rupert was really like.

Besides, having you nearby was enough. I could never have coped without the two of you."

This earned her another hug, before she waved her old friend goodbye. As the sun went down Lucy watched Freddie charge around the lawn with Pickle and his new puppy that he'd named Root in honour of his favourite cricketer. He seemed perfectly happy. When Jo had confirmed that the body was definitely Rupert, Lucy had taken him for a long walk down to the lake with the dogs. Her mouth had felt so dry as she tried to come up with the right words.

"You know we haven't seen Daddy for a long time," she'd begun. "Well, today I found out he died. I'm very sorry, darling."

She'd waited for some sort of reaction, but Freddie just continued throwing a stick for Pickle.

"Do you understand what that means, darling?" she'd asked gently.

"Does it mean he's not ever coming back?"

"Yes, it does."

"So, he won't hurt or upset you anymore?"

Lucy's throat had tightened. All this time she thought she'd hidden the worst of Rupert's actions from her son, but he'd known all along. She could only nod her head, not knowing what to say.

"Okay then," Freddie had said, so quietly she could hardly hear him.

Tilly padded out through the French doors now and flopped at her feet. Lucy reached down to stroke her.

"It's not easy being a mum, is it, old girl?" she said softly.

The French doors behind them had been fixed by Rob

and two of his workmen. Bill had let them in while Lucy had stayed upstairs, until they'd left. She hadn't seen Rob since that awful night with Guy. She'd barely seen anyone. All she'd wanted to do was hide away, avoiding the local gossip and the press with their long-lens cameras parked at the end of the driveway. Looking back, she wondered how she managed to get through those terrible twenty-four hours. Rupert's body being discovered while she was still reeling from the shock of learning that Guy had been stalking her. She kept reliving that night, torturing herself with thoughts of what might have happened if her friends hadn't turned up.

Rachel and Rob might have spoken in anger, but there was truth in what they'd both said. She'd always relied on someone else to solve her problems and take care of her. Always the same type too, a man with an air of authority, a charming smile, and not much else. She could never see through them until it was too late and, this time, she'd let a dangerous maniac get close to her and her little boy.

Well, no more. All she wanted to do now was concentrate on the estate. She had set a plan in motion to change Hartwell's fortunes and she was going to see it through. Despite all the dramas, enquiries and bookings had been flooding in, giving her something to focus on. For once Lucy agreed with Caroline—Freddie was all that mattered now, and she'd do everything she could to keep him safe and secure Hartwell's future.

In the distance, there was a faint rumble of thunder. Dark grey storm clouds were gathering over the moors, but Lucy didn't care. If it rained and the roof leaked and the buckets needed to be emptied, she would deal with it. She would deal with it all. Like Joan said, sometimes you needed a storm to clear your path.

The End

Don't miss the next book in The Secrets of Hartwell series, *Four Secrets Kept*!

Join Tule Publishing's newsletter for more great reads and weekly deals!

Acknowledgements

My thanks as always to the wonderful team at Tule:
Jane Porter,
Meghan Farrell, Cyndi Parent and Nikki Babri.
I was very lucky to work with three amazing editors again:
Sinclair Sawhney,
Helena Newton and Heidi Pergolski. Many thanks for all
your suggestions and your support.
A big thank you also to Lee Hyat for coordinating the
beautiful book cover design.

If you enjoyed *Four Hidden Treasures,*
you'll love the next books in…

The Secrets of Hartwell series

Book 1: *Four Hidden Treasures*

Book 2: *Four Secrets Kept*
Coming in May 2023

Book 3: *Four Silences Broken*
Coming in September 2023

Available now at your favorite online retailer!

More Books by H L Marsay

The Chief Inspector Shadow series

Available now at your favorite online retailer!

About the Author

H L Marsay always loved detective stories and promised herself that one day, she would write one too. She is lucky enough to live in York, a city full of history and mystery. When not writing, the five men in her life keep her busy – two sons, two dogs and one husband.

Thank you for reading

Four Hidden Treasures

If you enjoyed this book, you can find more from all our great authors at TulePublishing.com, or from your favorite online retailer.

TULE
PUBLISHING

Printed in Great Britain
by Amazon